T0026192

Last Stand in Lychford

LAST STAND IN LYCHFORD

PAUL CORNELL

A TOM DOHERTY ASSOCIATES BOOK

NEW YORK

LAST STAND IN LYCHFORD

Copyright © 2020 by Paul Cornell

Cover art by FORT

Edited by Lee Harris

A Tordotcom Book
Published by Tom Doherty Associates
120 Broadway
New York, NY 10271

www.tor.com

Tor® is a registered trademark of
Macmillan Publishing Group, LLC.

ISBN 978-1-250-75212-3 (ebook)
ISBN 978-1-250-75213-0 (trade paperback)

First Edition: November 2020

For Louise Bignell

Last Stand in Lychford

Prologue

THE REVEREND LIZZIE BLACKMORE was staring at the carnage in front of her. Or, she gradually realised, the *lack* of carnage. A few moments ago, the fairy prince Finn, who'd once been in some sort of ill-defined romantic relationship with her friend Autumn, had been in her kitchen at the Vicarage. He'd been on fire, but he'd been alive. Before Lizzie could react, however, before she could get her hands on the extinguisher or the fire blanket, he'd . . . exploded.

He'd exploded, and she'd thrown up her hands instinctively to protect her face, terrified in that second that she was going to die. The horrible adrenalin of that was still coursing through her.

But she'd realised the explosion hadn't hurt her, hadn't done anything to her. She'd lowered her hands. And now she could see what the explosion had done. At the centre of a very real pattern of burns on her kitchen tiles was lying . . . Finn's head. It lay on its side. There was no blood. His eyes were closed.

Oh God. Oh God.

With a great effort of will, she made herself squat down to look more closely, wondering if, as in a horror movie, his eyes were going to open again. They didn't.

"Finn?" she said, desperately. There was no reply. Of course there wasn't. The bottom of his neck was . . . smooth, sealed. There was just a base, like he was an action figure. The inside of his neck was dull gold, without any features, without organs. Feeling like she was in a dream, she reached out and touched it. It felt slightly rough. Almost like plastic. Or was that just a matter of associations on her part? Yes, because this didn't honestly feel like any material she'd ever touched.

She felt herself wobbling. What could she do for him? Nothing she could think of. He'd been blurting out some sort of warning.

She stood up. She wasn't going to cry. She wasn't. She started backing out of the kitchen. Her heel encountered something. She looked around.

There on the carpet lay Finn's hands. They were also both perfect. They were sealed at the wrists, golden inside.

Increasingly lost in the surreal, Lizzie looked around for more fairy body parts. She found, on the landing, part of his leg. It was still in a rounded section of what looked like leather trouser. It looked tailored, almost, to his current situation.

She took a deep breath and thought of her training, accessed that stoic part of her reserved for the most awful funerals. And the occasional wedding. She went to get her gardening gloves. She searched the house wearing them, and found the rest of the bits, handling them with the gloves as if she might disturb evidence in a police investigation that would surely never come to pass.

In the end, she was pretty satisfied that she'd found all of him. But what to do with him? She tried just holding the parts together, wondering if they'd somehow fuse and he'd come back to life. (She'd started with the thigh and calf to try to avoid the worst horrors of that.) It didn't happen. He was cold, she realised. Not like human corpses were cold, but like an object. The absence felt incidental, as if he could just be heated up again. But then, perhaps that was how those who weren't used to the dead felt about their dear departed. Lizzie was very used to the dead. The human dead.

Where could she put him? The kitchen table didn't seem respectful. She was thinking about Autumn now. About how she was going to break this news, what she'd have to show her. She decided it was going to be pretty awful no matter what or how. This purpose-built Vicarage had odd storage spaces here and there, including a room behind the room where the washing machine and drier were kept that contained nothing but an old broom and seemed to offer no suggestion as to what the space might be used for. So Lizzie now found a use for that room. A macabre one. Along its small collection of shelves she lined up what could only be described as pieces of fairy.

Then she called Autumn. She woke her up at half four. And, using the voice she kept for breaking bad news, she told her to prepare for a shock.

———————

An hour later, they both stood there in that little musty room, all the lights on, darkness still outside on this September morning, cups of strong, sweet tea in their hands, staring at what lay on the shelf.

"Are you sure that it's really him?" Autumn asked. She'd already touched his face. She'd done that immediately.

"He was talking to me before it happened. You always said there was an element of unreality about his nation, his people. When you went there, you said it was like a dream."

"A nightmare."

"It's almost as if when he comes here he's . . . a story. A prop in a movie."

Autumn put down her cup and went to touch one of the exposed gold surfaces. "Or maybe this is just what the attack or the blast or whatever that was did to him."

"I think you can call it an attack. He mentioned the fairy court and his father, as if something had happened to them. He said 'they' were going to bring the war here, that we were all ... going to die."

Autumn didn't even acknowledge the threat. "So we were right about there being some sort of conflict going on inside the land of fairy. Some sort of civil war. Fomented by the agents of Maitland Picton's 'people,' whoever they are. They want to annex fairy, then us." She stroked Finn's hair. "God, I was so fixated by him, then I was so scared of him. Then you and I started to treat him as some sort of annoying ..."

"That was mostly you."

Autumn looked momentarily guilty. "You joined in."

"I think he was a person. Of a sort that we hadn't really begun to understand. I'd say we should have a funeral, but the way those parts are, they sort of say to me ..."

"That he can be fixed."

"Yeah."

Autumn was silent for a moment. Then she seemed to decide she was going to say something. "Me and Luke ... we, err, got together."

Lizzie didn't know if she was meant to attempt surprise.

That was frankly a bit beyond her right now. "Finally."

"Before marriage. Couple of times. I hope that's okay." The look on her face was a mixture of nervousness and cheeky glow.

"I'm not judging. I hope *that's* okay. Was it . . . ?"

"Wow. Just wow. Leaving it at that."

That was obviously what Autumn had most wanted to tell her. "Really? You'll leave it at that?"

"Well, without drinks."

This was not the first time that Autumn had grandiosely failed to read the room when it was only her and Lizzie in it. Lizzie really wanted to say two things. *One:* that she was glad for Autumn, if tired by her continual assumption of puritanical judgment on Lizzie's part, but that maybe she could also consider how long Lizzie had been without romance in her life and . . . no, gah, that was unfair. Why was she feeling angry about this? Oh, possibly because of *two:* the pieces of fairy. "Autumn, was this really the best time—?"

"He doesn't look dead. He doesn't look real. I can't react to that. Not like I—"

"Sorry. Sorry."

"No. I'm sorry."

They looked at each other in silence for a moment. There was still an awkwardness between them. What was this about? Suddenly, as if her brain had said sod this,

Lizzie realised that a terrible joke had popped into her head. "Oh," she said. "No. I mustn't say it."

"What?"

"It's . . . awful. Just an awful joke."

"You always say people come out with awful jokes at funerals. And that it's healthy. And you just had a go at me for—"

"I did not—"

"And I'd really like to hear a normal reaction from you right now."

"Okay. I just thought . . ."

"Go on."

Lizzie looked helplessly at her, biting her lip. "The elf on a shelf."

Autumn managed a very solemn nod. "That is . . . indeed a terrible thing to say. You should be ashamed of yourself. Points will be taken off your vicar licence."

"I want to say Finn would have liked that. But I really don't think he would."

They both, finally, managed to laugh. Perhaps not as much as they could have. Still, the tension was punctured. A bit. Autumn hugged Lizzie. Lizzie held her, still aware of some little distance, some awkwardness entirely on her part that she hated and didn't want to acknowledge or understand. She squeezed. She didn't want Autumn feeling that emotion off her.

"Lizzie," whispered Autumn, "what are we going to do? I mean about . . . everything?"

"We'll work it out," said Lizzie. "It's not just us now." She hoped that sounded like she meant it.

1

THAT WAS HOW LYCHFORD came to be waiting.

Of course, that didn't mean Lizzie and Autumn had had that luxury. As people started waking up on the morning that Finn had exploded, Lizzie had begun phoning around or physically going to see every local organisation, explaining to them the warning that had been delivered to her, why it had been so urgent, and why they now needed to prepare for the worst.

She'd found that to be an unexpectedly terrible process. The people she spoke to had, these days, every reason to believe her. Everyone in the town had now shared in the waters of the well in the woods. They could all see the things that lay beyond the everyday, the things they had been protected from for so long. But more importantly, they could all now feel, with extra senses, the fragile nature of the now really pretty slight barriers around their little Cotswolds market town, behind which were other realities, with other inhabitants, some of whom had now declared they were coming to get them.

What took Lizzie by surprise was that, even though

they knew what Lizzie was talking about was real, they often still didn't want to know. Their nervousness at what she was telling them became, surprisingly quickly, irritation. They seemed to want her and Autumn to deal with it. One or two, by the end, Lizzie felt, had actively started to *blame* her for the situation.

"It's a bit much," said Sheila Parker, a widow from Prince Street who'd seemed affronted ever since she'd shared in the waters, probably because she'd always hated Lizzie's now deceased old friend Judith, the hedge witch, and positively disliked having new insight into what the old woman's point of view had been. "I mean, it shouldn't be up to us. We pay our rates."

Lizzie had had to suppress a desire, during that particular conversation, to say that she wasn't entirely sure the county council were up to funding the magical defence of all reality. And that if they were, being based in Gloucester, they had no more knowledge of the problem than anyone else who lived outside the bounds of Lychford itself.

She found, as she delivered her message in the next few days, this same negativity and deliberate obtuseness everywhere she went. It wasn't going to happen. It was somebody else's problem. Someone else would deal with it. Why wasn't Lizzie herself doing something?

Lizzie had expected the population to flee. She had

been comfortable with that. She and Autumn had already decided they could more easily defend the town, defend this focal point of all human reality, without worrying about saving innocent bystanders at the same time.

But no. These buggers, valuing the comfort of their lives over the continuing actuality of those lives, largely decided to stay put.

A few left—several of the younger folk with young families.

But in the next few weeks, to Lizzie's horror, those started *coming back*.

"Well," said Stacy Latislaw, who worked behind the counter at the town's third best charity shop, talking to Lizzie at her kitchen table. "Luna didn't really like it in Nantwich with my sister, and we thought, well, we can always leave again if whatever it is happens."

"Whatever it is," repeated Lizzie, numbly, sure that by now she was getting close to the end of her reserve of goodwill for the people of this town. She had preached from the pulpit, week after week, telling her congregation to leave. That was the opposite of everything the Church of England had trained her to do. They'd listened to her. They'd nodded. They'd stayed.

Lizzie had looked at the calm, placid face of Stacy Latislaw and thought of Richard Burton's narration at the start of *Jeff Wayne's Musical Version of The War of the*

Worlds, and she wanted to swear at her. She wanted to run into the marketplace and bellow, "They're coming!"

Perhaps there were some good reasons for this urge to stay put. Perhaps some of it was down to the fact that nobody outside of Lychford would believe or understand the reasons why anyone inside it had left.

Or perhaps the people of this town were just stupid, complacent sheep who loved their comfortable lives so much they hadn't noticed the slaughterhouse in the next field.

Lizzie had struggled with her faith in God before. But all her extraordinary training in the ways of human life hadn't prepared her to so lose her faith in *people.*

She decided, a couple of weeks into the waiting, to instead turn her focus to the town's organisations. And, of course, the committee members of all of them had looked seriously at her and had nodded and agreed, and then things . . . a few things . . . had actually started to happen. The Women's Institute, who were already doing a sort of neighbourhood watch scheme for the homes on the edge of town, had organised "magical self-defence" courses in which the (all organically sourced and fair trade guaranteed) protective charms Autumn had recommended were mass produced in jam jars and everyone was instructed in their use. The History Society had got their members to seek out useful occult books. (So far, according to Autumn, they had found one and a half, whatever that meant, and neither the one nor the half were any use.) The Festival committee were staging regular open mic nights at the Plough, which had seemed a strange response, but perhaps the best they could do.

The University of the Third Age had even invited Lizzie to speak to at one of their meetings at the Fincham Hall. She realised about a minute into what she'd planned as a talk about looking out for strange beings in one's garden and putting extra magical defences around one's house that members of the elderly audience were talking over what she was trying to say, calling out the refrain she was getting used to: if this was so important, why wasn't *she* doing something about it? Why wasn't that coloured girl at the magic shop doing something about it?

Lizzie wanted to walk off there and then. She got to the end of her piece. But she didn't take audience questions. She'd already heard enough.

Perhaps there was one sign that, at least on some level, the locals were taking this threat seriously. Autumn's magic shop, Witches, gradually became, in the weeks since the message, a centre of the town's conversations, a place people went to like a favourite news website when they needed reassurance, when they needed grounding in tense times. But having too many customers to deal with on her own was, for Autumn, a completely new and rather taxing experience. Especially when they largely wanted nothing *but* reassurance. Especially when she was at the same time working out how to defend the town and how to bring a fairy back from the dead. She'd put up a card in the window of the supermarket, seeking an assistant, but hadn't had any applicants. "They think," she'd said to Lizzie, "it means they'd also have to, you know, defend against the dark arts. And that is something, as we've discovered, that they absolutely do not want to do."

Lizzie felt that she hadn't even begun to describe to her friend the despair she'd started to feel. There was still a distance between them, and she had no idea why. "I'm so scared for them," she said. "And for us. I don't know what they'll do if and when anything actually shows up."

"*When*," Autumn had said.

The truth of which led to another source of dismay. Lizzie found that her email backlog began to again contain an increasing number of mundane matters. People were still dying, of course, baptisms were on the rise, and people from the town were once more feeling able to get married in her church. Her church wardens were starting to talk about preparing for Christmas.

"What the hell," she said as she stared at the screen one evening. "We are the turkeys, and we are voting for Christmas."

She was pretty sure that this state of complete denial

and refusal to prepare was exactly what their enemy, whatever it was, wanted.

———————

Autumn Blunstone sat behind the counter in her magic shop, looking at the stool where Judith Mawson used to sit. It wasn't opening time yet. But already customers had appeared outside, nervously hanging about. She had regulars now. People who regularly wasted her time, that was. Who would have thought that, running a shop, she'd have to put up with the general public? She had a duty to serve them, but she didn't feel up to it yet today, despite several coffees, so she was leaving it until she had no choice. She had a horrible weight in her head, made up of a sort of distant, complicated grief for Finn and a solid continuing grief for Judith, and also the fear that she didn't have time for either. The lack of urgency on the part of the townsfolk that Lizzie kept anxiously reporting made her feel more urgent. How could the locals be like this? How could you fail to change, when you had this sudden awareness of where you actually stood in the cosmic scheme of things? She supposed it was like that line from *Spinal Tap*. There was such a thing as *too much* fucking perspective.

So it was all going to come down to just the two of

them, wasn't it? And it didn't help that Lizzie was acting all weird since Autumn had told her about Luke. It had been a mistake to mention the sex. Still, she hadn't anticipated this level of . . . whatever it was.

No. She had to concentrate. The weeks of waiting were ticking away toward . . . what? When would "they" come? To be something solid that she could fight?

Weeks ago, Autumn had put the . . . pieces of Finn . . . in several bags and carried them to her shop. They were now in a cupboard in the work room. She had tried to research the problem, had tried some divinations, but she hadn't found any answers.

Luke, since he'd gained extra senses like the rest of the town had, had spent hours with her in that work room. He'd been delighted with immersing himself in the details of her world. She'd been in turns pleased about that and then perversely irritated by the strength of his interest. This was her thing. In the end, it was her responsibility. And he'd been neglecting his own work. Almost uniquely, in this stupid town.

The doorbell rang. Again. And it still wasn't opening time. Autumn tiredly looked over, but saw Sunil Mehra, the pensioner who ran the town's Indian restaurant. He was carrying a shopping bag. He had on his face a look of sadness and anger that he was just about containing.

Oh God. Sunil hadn't been here for Judith's funeral,

hadn't been here for the rain.

Autumn quickly got to her feet, unlocked the door, and let him in. "Sunil, I'm so sorry, we tried to find you."

"I'm sure you did. This is what I get for going on holiday with no phone. I knew she was old. I knew . . . please, what *happened* to Judith? And what are my staff telling me about this . . . rain? Why has everyone lost their marbles?"

Autumn closed the shop again and led him into the back room. This was going to be a difficult conversation.

Her name was Zoya Boyko, and she was desperate. She was desperate as she walked her daughter, Jas, to school that morning, through the lovely streets of the market town, past the lovely fields of the Cotswolds, holding her daughter's hand, repeating all the things she liked to repeat. "*Go Jetters* go, go go go. We need to go to school. *Go Jetters* go, Mummy!"

"*Go Jetters* go," Zoya said, keeping her voice upbeat. Jas couldn't pick up on how a lot of other people felt, but she usually could tell, immediately and deeply, when Mummy was showing signs of worry, of weakness. The little girl would fret about it, maybe melt down, might not even get to school, and today Zoya really needed

Jas to get to school. They walked through riches, every morning, past houses with gates and driveways. They weren't part of what they walked through. Zoya and Jas lived in "the backs" of Lychford, in a room in a flat, rented out by Mitch, who was nice enough, but who had troubles of his own. If Zoya couldn't find the money to pay his rent this month, as he'd told her when she'd been a week late last time, he'd straight away have to find someone to take her place. He had a mortgage to pay.

The job at the shop wouldn't get her enough, not after the days off she'd had to take for her daughter. She wasn't on the sort of contract where they'd pay her for time off, and nor would she ever be, not with Jas. This month she'd be about fifty pounds short. What could she sell that'd be worth fifty pounds? But she couldn't sell something every month. She'd already started looking for a cheaper place, but there was nowhere that cheap, not around here, where Jas's dad had brought them and left them. And Jas was so settled in the school here, actually making progress, changing for the better for the first time, thanks to her wonderful teaching assistant, Charlie. They couldn't lose that. Zoya wouldn't *let* her lose that.

She made herself think about lunch. Lunch was when Zoya had an hour to herself and could read her books. She didn't like to buy them, not even from charity shops, so she was making her way through everything Mum had left her. She wasn't sure if some of them were stories or meant to be real, but they made her head spin, took her away from here. On some mornings when she walked the complicated way in to school that Jas insisted on, she ended up thinking about what she read, and for a while she could ignore the money sitting all around her and felt instead the world tipped at an angle, like people were watching, good people, from places above her and under her, from horizons she couldn't see. It was as if part of her was being kept from her, kept in safety, just over there. Just beyond her reach. Some days it felt like a specific place, like she could turn her head until she was facing it and walk there, somewhere just to the north. It was like the feeling when she'd been at university and a new term was starting, that feeling of being about to learn, about to grow, about to see that new horizon.

She liked all these feelings, they were the only comfort she had, but they also scared her, because they were yet another sign of how apart she was from these townsfolk. How weird was the pressure making her, how much was she losing it because of how things were around here? In the last few weeks, a collective insanity seemed to have gripped this weird, privileged, English place. Everyone was talking about magic. Everyone was saying there had been a rain, a rain which had somehow penetrated through roofs and windows, that had given everyone the power to feel something they had not previously felt. These people were all boasting about it, and all nervous about it at the same time. It was like they'd gained yet another special level of privilege. Like they'd all been given a new leaf blower or something. But they seemed to expect it to be taken from them, or expected to have to pay for it, for once in their lives, and that thought scared them, so they didn't accept it, they moved swiftly on.

Many of them talked about seeing weird or wonderful things. They'd suddenly point, look, on the hillside over there! But there was never anything to be seen. And then they'd say no, there couldn't have been anything, not to worry.

These English were crazy.

But also it was all like a fairy tale from the town where Zoya had been born, from Odessa in the Ukraine. It was the sort of nonsense her grandma would have come out with, that her mother had told Zoya was all right in its place, but not to talk to other children about, because it might make them laugh at her family. But here, now, the school had even been talking about it in assembly. They had scared Jas for nothing, for this collective power trip. But, no, she mustn't think badly of them, even that couldn't take away how much they'd done for the little girl.

Oh God, they were both stuck between so many things.

Zoya had been in town when this rain was supposed to have come. She had been getting Jas ready for school as usual that morning. She had put her hand out, felt the drops, decided on a hooded coat for her daughter. It had taken her a while to even remember these everyday events when people had started spouting this bullshit. There had been no great revelation for her, no feeling of being able to see new things. Perhaps this was a Brexit thing, magic only for the *real* British! Zoya wondered as she got to the school gates if perhaps there was something concrete behind it all, pesticides in the air or something, a mass delusion, and the wind had just been in the wrong direction for her house. But the first she'd heard about any of this had been from her neighbours, so the wind seemed to have been pretty selective. And now she thought of that, she was worrying about Jas having breathed it in. On top of everything else. Her daughter's lack of communication was such that it would be hard to tell if she had. It wasn't like Zoya was going to start asking her about something that could scare her so much.

"Please take one." That was Mrs. Cotton, the deputy head, who was standing at the gate, giving out sheets of paper to all the parents.

Zoya took the piece of paper as she ushered Jas into the playground and read it as her daughter dutifully went to stand in line, ahead of all the other children, who were still playing. The paper was a list of forthcoming meetings about "the new situation."

She felt so angry. All the time. This delusion again. When she couldn't afford her rent. Could she maybe make some money by telling a newspaper about this? It didn't seem likely. It was all too odd. She could hear herself saying the words: "These bloody English seem to believe..." But how many of these newspapers would listen to her after she'd started like that, even? The stupidity, the dividing nonsense that had driven her from where she'd grown up, had followed her here. It had stuck her here. There was no learning to be had, not like she dreamed about. There was instead a lack of it, a turning away from it. And there seemed to be nothing she could do to make a better life for herself and her daughter, no way to get away from it. Something, surely, had to change.

She glared at the teacher, crumpled up the paper, and went to join Jas at the line.

———————————

Lizzie had just got up from her desk at the Vicarage after having a hack at her ridiculously mundane email backlog and was on her way to get a strong cup of flavoured coffee, when her phone rang. "Listen, it's err... nobody wanted to bother you, but . . . I think there might be, I mean I know you've been saying something might be going to happen and, sorry, trying to speak around my new false teeth . . ."

Lizzie recognised the voice of Lydia Bates, one of her congregation, but just as she was about to ask what was going on, she heard the phone on the other end being taken, perhaps forcibly, by another hand.

"We can't get out of town," said Carrie Anne Christopher, the chair of the Lychford Festival.

"What?" said Lizzie, feeling a sudden awful chill in her stomach.

"It's just started, just this last few minutes. I wanted to go to the garage to get a few bits, but there's this . . . something. I can't explain it. We're on the hill at the top of London Road. I'm going to try to get a bit closer. There are lots of people here. Oh. Oh God. It's horrible. You have to come. Sorry, I have to deal with things here." And she rang off.

Lizzie tried Autumn, left a voicemail message, then called Shaun, Judith's police officer son. "I'm already heading over," he said, his voice sounding like he was running, "but I can't get any backup. I can't seem to get reception for any calls outside the town. Meet you there, Reverend."

Lizzie grabbed her coat and ran out of the house.

London Road was a one-way route out of town that had been the best Lychford could do in terms of traffic calming. It was wooded on both sides, forested inclines leading down to the road as it made its way uphill. As she approached, she could see cars backed up all along the road. The drivers had mostly got out to talk to each other.

"Shaun jogged through here a few minutes ago," called a young man Lizzie recognised as Chris the builder, who was still in the cab of his van. "He said he'd told the ones at the back to turn around and go home, but nothing's changing, so maybe more have joined them. And listen to this." He switched on his cab radio and turned up the volume so Lizzie could hear. It was just static, wherever he went on the dial. "Nothing on the digital either," he said. "So, this is probably nothing to worry, right?"

"No," said Lizzie, unable to stop herself from letting her pent-up irritation show, "no, it probably is something to worry about."

Chris's dad, Paul, stepped out of the other door of the van and came around to see her, a look of urgent concern on his face. She was aware that a crowd was gathering, looking to her. "Is this it, then?" said Paul. "Is this them?"

"It could well be," said Lizzie. "I won't know until I get to the front."

She marched off before they could start offering everyday alternatives for what it might be. She was distantly pleased to sense a number of them follow her.

Some of the drivers the crowd passed, mostly the ones who'd stayed with their vehicles, were laughing or just annoyed, carefree compared to the more complicated, anxious verging on guilty reactions of the locals. These were the ones who'd been caught in the jam when they were just passing through town, she guessed. There was quite a division between the locals and those from outside.

Finally, they got to the front of the traffic jam, near the top of the hill, where Carrie Anne and Mrs. Caversham-Thoroughgood of the Women's Institute were trying to hold back a growing crowd of people who were variously annoyed, disputing, starting to get scared. Most of them stepped back to let Lizzie pass, leaving a few, the non-locals, to stare in puzzlement at what a vicar might be bringing to this situation. "Let her through," called Mrs. Caversham-Thoroughgood, her voice commanding with the volume required of a hundred junior gymkhanas.

"Thank God you're here," said Carrie Anne. "I think this might be it."

Lizzie was grateful to find one of the few people who'd taken her warnings to heart right at the centre of this. "Thank you," she said. "What's going on?"

"A lot of weirdness," said Carrie Anne. "Your department. Shaun's on top of it as much as anyone is."

Lizzie saw that Shaun, in uniform but as always looking slightly out of his depth, was laying out cones across the road. Up ahead, in front of the line he'd already put down, a small car was steaming in the middle of the tarmac. It seemed to have been cut in two just back from its bonnet. The front half, which lay several feet down the road, seemed to have a small electrical fire going on. But what immediately stood out was the person inside. Half of him was lying forward against the steering wheel in the front half of the car, a mass of blood. She could see through the back window of the rear half that the rest of the man was slumped back against his seat. There was just enough of a human shape left to ascertain that he'd been cut in half along with his vehicle.

Lizzie crossed herself and muttered a prayer for the man and for all their protection. The crowd shouldn't be seeing this. But maybe it was what they needed. "What did this?" she asked.

"No idea," said Shaun, coming over. "But whatever it is, it's still there. Look." He picked up a branch from the road and threw it. It cracked backward toward him when it hit a point near the bisection of the car and driver. It landed back at his feet, smashed into pieces.

The crowd cried out. The noise children make when they're suddenly, genuinely scared. Behind that sound, immediately drowning it out, there were angry shouts too. A lack of understanding from the out of towners.

Someone had started to sob.

"Looks deliberate," said Matty from the yard, who was sitting on the front bumper of his concrete mixer lorry. There was a distant, empty look on his face. "I mean, I were right behind him. I saw something I couldn't really see but that I could, you know, feel, come down from above him, straight through. Like an axe coming down. I slammed on the brakes, or I'd have been right into it. Fuck of a coincidence—sorry, Vicar—if he'd just happened to be there when it zapped down, like. For it to start up or appear or whatever just as he went through. When he were just on that line." He shook his head. "This one behind me nearly ran into me."

"But I didn't," said a lorry driver with a Dutch accent. "What is this? Why the vicar?" Lizzie pushed back the silly annoyance she always felt about people apologising for swearing when she was around. And she mustn't be all high and mighty about these people being forced to deal with what they'd refused to acknowledge before. They were going to need to pull together, and quickly.

"What can you see here?" she pointed to the road and listened as the Dutch driver described the scene pretty much as they could see it. Except what he'd seen of the accident itself had made him think a tree had fallen. He was, however, puzzled about where that tree was now. He couldn't feel anything in the air in front of him, like Lizzie could now that she'd been told something was there, but yes, he had seen the branch fly backward and smash. He now thought this was probably some sort of secret weapon test. He had many ideas about how this connected to various conspiracy theories he'd heard about.

Lizzie recognised a non-rained-on mind struggling to deal with the realities of life in Lychford. That was to be expected. At least he and the others like him weren't likely to try to walk through this invisible wall. She looked back to the crowd. "Did anyone know the victim?"

"It's Lacey Beresford's lad," said Paul, quietly. "He'd have been off to work at Mott's farm."

There was a general murmur of grief. Lizzie had to put that aside for the moment. "We should see how far this wall goes," she said.

Several of them went with her, and several more headed off the other pavement, so they went up into the woods on both sides. The locals were talking and talking, still trying to deflect the reality of this, some of them even starting to agree with that truck driver, despite what they knew, despite what they could *feel*. Lizzie discovered that this cutting line was marked in the woods by sliced rows of trees, some of them bisected, each half of them having fallen in a different direction. At least it was pretty easy to see where the wall was. "Just as well," said

Shaun when she shared that thought aloud, "I don't have enough cones."

They kept walking, a hundred metres or so. The wall continued all the way along. The smell of cut timber was everywhere on the wind. A text from Carrie Anne in the other party confirmed that it kept going in the other direction too. Lizzie brought up Google Maps to check her suspicions. Only the saved version was available, nothing from the server outside the town, but it was enough to confirm that the wall was an arc, part of a circle.

She and those with her jogged back to the crowd at the traffic jam. The locals and outsiders were arguing now, fear turning into anger. She shouted for them to listen. They all turned to look at her, the locals telling those from outside to shut up. "This is enemy action," she said. "This is what we've been telling you about. They've locked us in."

————————

It had taken an hour and three cups of tea, and Autumn had purposefully ignored all the urgent noises coming from her phone while the conversation was going on, but at the end of it, Sunil seemed to understand what she was trying to tell him. He let out a long breath. "This explains a lot," he said. "This is definitely what my staff now believe every word of. I suppose I believe it too. What choice do I have? It's everything Judith always talked about, all of which I assumed was metaphor, or old age. I just wish . . ." He put a hand to his brow and took a moment to control himself. "I wish I had been here for her funeral. I wish I could have said goodbye."

Autumn took his hand. "She was brilliant at the end. She never stopped being amazing."

"I had . . . backed off a little. Let her be. The number of times I saw her and she clearly didn't know who I was. It's like I lost the woman I . . . I was friends with, I suppose. It never came to more than that. I lost her months ago. And yet I just don't know, I feel a gap. I want a conversation I will never now be able to have."

"Yeah."

They were both silent together for a while. When he spoke again, it was with fear in his voice. "These terrible things, they defy rationality. They seem outside of science."

"They're not. I won't let myself think they are."

"I knew Judith worked for you, so I suppose I suspected, this shop being what it is, that you'd know . . . anyway, that's why I decided we should have this conversation, and why I should bring this to you." He reached into the bag he'd brought with him and pulled out a round shape, about the size of a cricket ball, wrapped in newspaper and string. Autumn's extra senses felt something uneasy about the bundle, something negative, but it was such a small feeling. It was like something was waiting to be hatched, like inside the bundle was some sort of . . . egg? "It seems while I was away this arrived by post at the restaurant. I opened it up, but . . . well, I don't know what this is."

Autumn still felt profoundly odd making a magical sign of protection openly in front of someone. Sunil just raised an eyebrow at it, interested. She went and got some of the holy water Lizzie had given her a supply of, and her own protective unguent (mostly Aldi "light in colour" olive oil) and drew a circle on the table around the package. Then she untied the package and opened it up. It was highly unlikely Judith would have sent something dangerous to someone she cared about, but as Sunil had said, toward the end she'd done some very random shit.

On the paper lay something that should have been in a butcher's shop. Or no . . . more like an archaeological dig. It was an organ of some kind, though none that Autumn recognised. It was brown and ancient, parched of the liquids that had stained it. But it wasn't mummified or preserved. It had that egg sensation about it, that here was something that still contained potential.

"Is it a heart?" asked Sunil.

"Romantic gesture," said Autumn, and immediately regretted it.

But Sunil smiled sadly. "There was no note. Perhaps this is something sent from her dementia, something taken from an animal. A sacrifice? Something to protect me? Or perhaps there's no meaning to it."

Autumn told him she'd look into it. Sunil seemed satisfied, took her hand again, looked awkward, again with that feeling of incompletion, of not knowing. Finally, he headed out. Autumn stretched, sighed, picked up her phone and glanced at it. And let out a scream.

Ten minutes later, Lizzie looked around to see Autumn skidding to a halt. "We're going to need you to start answering your phone," she said, and immediately regretted it.

"It was something important. What, did you think I was with Luke?"

Lizzie was incredibly aware that they had an audience. "Tabling that," she said. "And sorry. This is the problem we're facing."

Thankfully, Autumn nodded and listened. "Why were you able to text me?" was the first thing she asked.

"Sorry?" said Lizzie.

"Radio stations aren't getting in, and neither is the radio for the phones. It's not as if we've got a mobile phone tower nearby, and even if we did, it would need to communicate with other towers. So that's got to be deliberate. Whatever this is is letting us talk to each other, but not to the world."

Together with a number of, now highly engaged, locals, they headed to check out the rest of what seemed to be a circular wall. They first went to the Folly, the pub at the end of the road going out of town to the north. This was the route that went over the bridge on the river that had given the town its name. Developing as a market town dependent on the wool trade, roads roughly at the compass points had evolved to bring sheep flocks in from outlying farms, and that was the way it had stayed. Now each one of the roads, according to reports, were bisected by the invisible wall. In this particular case it was marked by a line of stones that Erica, the landlady of the Folly, had placed there. She and her family had heard about what was going on from a sobbing friend on the eastern side of town and had rushed out into the road to halt approaching vehicles. Luckily, this road was the one with the least traffic. So this was the only access point where the arrival of the wall hadn't resulted in damage either to people or vehicles. Jake Beresford had so far been the only fatality. On the other side of the invisible wall here at the bridge there was already a queue of vehicles, with people at the back continually coming forward and having to test the wall for themselves, despite being yelled at by Erica's two burly sons.

"Maybe I should have put the cones here," said Shaun.

"I think that's right about them killing someone deliberately," said Autumn. "Them being whichever power set this up. They had to throw this whole wall . . . I guess it goes all the way up?"

"It seems to," said Lizzie. "One of the senior school kids sent up a drone and it exploded."

"They had to put it all up at once, so they targeted one person, waited until he was in the way and left what happened on the other roads to chance. Maybe Jake was a sacrifice to help power this thing."

"The outside world," said Lizzie, "will now be aware of what's going on. And they will be very puzzled."

"So the enemy really don't care if they're seen doing this. It's all out in the open now. An attack on the whole of reality. Like Maitland Picton's mission was meant to be."

"Which helps us not at all. Even if the army shows up. We can't even get a message out. Not until they're within shouting distance, anyway. Because at least sound is getting through."

"Judith left something that might be useful. But she

didn't leave it with us."

Lizzie was surprised to hear about Judith's strange parcel. "It can't be relevant. If Judith had been aware this was going to happen she'd have said something."

"True. But we were all aware of the general fairy-political situation, her included. She'd have assumed we were going to be dealing with the rebel fairies at some point. I just don't know why she would have kept the heart or whatever it is from us. I already tried it on the pieces of Finn, by the way, I took just a moment to do that before I came over—" Her tone had already become defensive.

"Right. I'd have done that too."

"—and like you, I assumed that somehow Judith knew the future. But rubbing it on the pieces, squeezing it over them. . . . No. I do not think she divined that Finn was going to explode and might need healing."

Shaun came back over. "I'm going to get anyone stuck on this side to leave their vehicles and head back into town. I've sent a couple of the burlier lads to head out to the other compass point roads and do the same. I think the best thing I can do is keep checking up on those compass points. Okay with you two?"

Lizzie looked to Autumn, saw her nod absently, still annoyed. Those new to Lychford would find a welcome in the town's three cash-strapped coffee houses. For those businesses there was definitely a silver lining. "Yes," she said.

"You two are going to sort this out, aren't you?" said Shaun. "Quickly? Because—"

"Thank you, Shaun," said Lizzie, actually finding it in herself to dismiss a police officer.

Shaun paused for a moment, then decided to let himself be dismissed. But the look on his face said his urgent question wasn't going to go away.

"So," said Autumn, "no pressure."

———————

Zoya was having a perplexing morning working in the shop, listening while trying not to to the increasingly bizarre and scared stories the locals were telling each other. It seemed that nobody had left for work this morning, that they all thought there was some sort of wall stopping them from getting out of Lychford. Was there not a podcast documentary series to be made about this? The town that lost its marbles. "Logan," she said to the boy who was on the tills with her, "why do people here believe all this mime artiste bullshit?"

He stared at her. "Oh my God. Weren't you here when it rained? My nan wasn't here, either, but when she came back there was still a bit of the water around and she must have inhaled it or whatever and now she can feel it, too, just like the rest of us can."

Zoya made a heroic effort and contained her exasperation. "This feeling . . . is it like perhaps someone nice is looking down on the town from the north and he wants everything to be well and there's maybe another bit of you, a good bit, that needs to learn, out there somewhere? I feel that, a little, sometimes. This is me being charitable. This is a slight poetic moment. This is the closest I can get to why everyone here is now bugfuck crazy in the head."

Logan stared at her. "No, it's not like that at all."

"Ah well. I thought it was worth a try."

Logan's phone buzzed and he pulled it out to look at it. He became immediately agitated. "The boss says if we think there's any danger, we should pull down the shutters and close up. Are you feeling any danger?"

"No."

"I am a bit. Maybe not enough? A bit, though."

Zoya felt that perhaps engagement would stop him from jittering back and forth between the tills. "Tell me more about this feeling of yours. How everyone feels."

Autumn and Lizzie had headed back to Autumn's shop, aware of townsfolk heading home all around them. "So what's the enemy's next move?" Autumn asked, unlocking the door of her business. God, they'd been used to the town not knowing or caring about what they did. She'd been used to the pressure of saving the universe, but everyone down the pub knowing about it? That made everything gibberingly more enormous. And Lizzie continuing to be off with her was exactly what she didn't need right now.

"Finn said they were 'coming,' so, having cut us off, that may be the next thing. We should put everyone on alert." As they went inside, Lizzie showed Autumn a list of local resources on her phone, from the care workers at the retirement home to the library staff.

"I don't know how much help local anything is going to be," said Autumn. "They're already starting to panic."

"But we have to warn people what to expect."

"Yes. Of course. I'm just saying—"

"Finn thought you could do something about whatever this is. Those were his last words, that I should go and get you."

"Thanks for that." Autumn headed in the direction of the kettle. She'd decided the only way to tackle Lizzie about something that was getting to her was, as always, head on. "Okay, there's time for this now. We need to be on the same page. What's getting to you? Is it something about Luke?" She looked over her shoulder to see that Lizzie had immediately folded her arms. Which was a sure sign something was about to blow. "We shouldn't have shagged, is that it?"

The expression on Lizzie's face did not become in any way more peaceful.

———————

Logan had been describing his personal odyssey with his new senses, at some length. Which seemed at least to be calming him down. A little. "It isn't what you said about someone nice looking down on us. It's about terrible things lurking around everywhere. And the boss says now they've walled us all in. With them inside, too, probably. Lurking."

"I think your version is what isn't true. This is fertiliser-based weirdness everyone is deluded from."

"Deluded? You're the one who's weird."

"Why do you say this?"

"Because ours is all of us, and yours is just you."

"Ah. Now that's more what I'm used to."

"What's that supposed to mean?"

Zoya was grateful at that moment for the bell signifying the arrival of a customer. It was an old lady, who immediately started yelling at them. "We've been told to go to our homes! By the police! It's happening!" And then she ran out again.

Logan, galvanised, went to the door, fumbled with the latches, seemed to realise he was too panicked to handle anything so fiddly, and with a little cry, fled off through the shop, presumably aiming for the back door. Which made no sense. Because that old lady had been fine.

Zoya wouldn't have said she was calm, exactly, in the face of all this, but she wasn't terrified either. She had, in her life, seen some stuff. "Decadent," she muttered to herself. She would lock up and take what she was now pretty sure was an official day off with pay, the first task of which would be to head over to the school to make sure Jas wasn't in the way of any of this insanity.

She went to the door. She realised that the marketplace outside was weirdly silent. She opened the door and looked out. Yup. Deserted. Everyone was taking this order pretty damn seriously. But then, that one police officer who was sometimes in the town was as cuckoo as all the rest. She closed the door again, drew the bolts, and found the latches for the shutters that had so defeated Logan.

———

Lizzie was about to let out all her tension by finally bellowing . . . she didn't know what she was going to bellow but her cheeks were flushed and she was certainly deeply

upset about something and here it was, the big something she'd say that would let the row start to happen and
then maybe she'd find out why—

But then something shot past her cheek and was suddenly in the wall beside Autumn.

"Get down!" Autumn shouted, throwing herself to the
floor.

Lizzie tried to do the same. But as she did so, there was
a sudden, impossible pain in her shoulder and the impact
of it spun her around. She fell, tripping over her feet. As
she hit the ground the pain in her shoulder exploded.

It was more pain than she had ever felt before. She had
a moment to realise that.

And then she was lost.

2

AUTUMN LAY ON THE FLOOR, panting. She looked to where the . . . arrow, yes it was an arrow, or at least it was a transparent shaft with blue liquid inside . . . was embedded in the wall. It glowed in her extra senses, with the malice of a vicious snake. Another, exactly the same, but without its contents, was in Lizzie's shoulder, where she was lying on the ground, completely still. From where Autumn was, she couldn't even see if she was breathing. Her face now had a tinge of blue to it. Poison arrows. Shit.

She looked to the windows and found no holes, certainly none in the direction the arrows had come from. So these bloody things had come straight through the wall. She wasn't safe wherever she was. But presumably they still needed a line of sight to locate her, or—

Two more arrows shot close over her head and hit the wall beside the first.

Right. They were firing blind. And there were at least two archers. She reached out a toe toward the inner door and kicked at it, so hard it hit the frame and quickly rebounded back to close itself. A flurry of arrows went through the wall and the door and, she could hear, embedded themselves somewhere in her work room. Autumn stayed put. A few moments later, there were more distant thuds. They'd heard the sound, thought she'd gone in there, and moved round the building to fire blind into that space with no windows.

They obviously could decide which surfaces their arrows went through. Bloody hell.

She had a few moments now. What could she do with them?

She slid over to Lizzie and found that yes, she was breathing, just about. Regularly too. This had always been Autumn's nightmare: having to get medical attention for a supernatural problem.

So, save the vicar, save the world. In that order, probably. But first Autumn had to save herself. What would Judith have done? Complain. Yes, thank you, brain, but after that? All of Autumn's major resources were in her work room. She needed to put up some sort of protection around the shop. Something strong. That would need the calling down of power. That was going to require sacrifice.

Okay, who was the most beloved and powerful entity that Autumn could think of right now? Oh. Oh shit, this felt like blasphemy. Lizzie might well see it as that, though she distantly remembered Lizzie saying something about how she didn't believe in blasphemy. Which made no sense. Well, anyway, Lizzie wasn't conscious right now. So . . .

"Judith, I call on you as an intercessional presence," Autumn whispered, putting every ounce of emotion she had into the words. And that was plenty. All she had to do was look at Lizzie and it was plenty. "I call on you as a god made of my need, my desperate need. Please Judith, mother to us all, see us and help us today and focus this sacrifice." And as she said the words, she found gestures, born of her research and her emotion, that let her shape what she was willing into being out there into something that was in here. The shape of the sounds, the shape of her hands, the emotional content of the phrases, it was all working, she could feel it was, to make her will real in the world. But now she had to commit. Now she had to find something to give to her higher purpose, to this higher power she'd conjured up from the depths of her imagination, which were also the depths of reality.

What could she give that Judith would ever approve of? Not blood. Too messy. Too vital to continuing life, and Judith had always been about that. It couldn't be anything dark either. Judith had always been a hedge witch, the local wise woman. She'd used the power of the dark once, in that she'd pursued selfish and aggressive ends, and she'd regretted it enormously. The goal here was fierce maternal protection. Of which Autumn didn't have much personal experience. The sacrifice had to be something that had fondness to it.

She knew what it had to be. She slid quickly across the floor again, got to the counter, and pulled out a drawer from underneath, brought it to the ground as silently as she could, because the noises of impact had ceased from the other room and the assassins must be trying to work out where she was.

Why hadn't they come straight in through the door?

Because they were being cautious. They must think she had some way of hurting them. Well, she wished she knew what they were worried about. But in the meantime . . . her hands found the emergency tea bags.

She ripped them open, threw the leaves onto the floor, and made them into a protective pattern that matched the intensity of her emotion and the flavour of the being she'd called up, this gorgeous Judith who had none of the awkward side to her that . . .

No.

Autumn made a tiny adjustment to her pattern, to her thoughts, and to the words she'd started whispering again. There couldn't be any lies in this fond device. "Judith, you tough old bat, bring protection to us now. You never really told us, but I know you loved us, and we love you now. By the power of all you were to us, Judith—"

She heard the door open. She could feel who it was without having to chance looking. Killers. Intent and calm. They were taking a risk now. Or maybe wondering if they'd brought their prey down. They felt like something out of a story, in a way which she'd never felt about Finn. There was something ... dreamlike about them. But also they were death that would be upon her in a second.

If she wasn't a badass witch. "Get out of my house!" she bellowed. And she completed the pattern in shape and sound and thought as she did so.

The door slammed shut, and she felt two beings go flying. They landed too far away for her to sense. Maybe all the way out of this world. Maybe not.

Autumn leapt to her feet, made herself take a moment to thank Judith, then went straight to Lizzie and started to make her comfortable. There wasn't much point in dialing 999. The paramedics wouldn't get through the wall. And even if the local first responders got here, there wouldn't be much they could do for Lizzie. No, that was going to be down to Autumn, and whatever she could find out about the blue stuff in that arrow.

Lizzie woke up.

She wasn't in Autumn's shop anymore. Oh God. She had opened her eyes and she was somewhere completely different. She had woken up from her life. Did that mean she was dead?

She sat up and looked around. She was in an oddly simple space, a black void that had . . . angular areas, places of light and shade, as if she was in a dense forest of shapes that went not up and down like trees, but in all directions.

She got to her feet and found that gravity wasn't exactly where she expected it to be. She stumbled, nearly fell, managed to right herself at what felt like a new angle from where she'd been lying. Her eyes were adjusting now. The shapes around her were getting better defined. She reached out and touched one of them. The black surface stretched high off above her, lost in darkness, and also somehow below her as well. It fell like there were precipices all around.

Shit. What was this place?

She took some hesitant steps forward, wary of falling, but found, somehow, a surface all around her. What were her extra senses saying? That they couldn't offer her any more help than her regular ones could. This place felt very dull to them, very empty. Oh. If hell was being kept from the presence of God . . . no, she mustn't think like that. If this was hell, it was at least at body temperature, she wasn't in pain, she could breathe, and the air smelled like . . . no, she had no point of reference for whatever that smell was. That frightened her in a way she'd never experienced before. So there were even new experiences to be had.

There was a vague light ahead. She came to some sort of gap and realised she was looking at something she recognised.

She was looking down on Lychford. It was night down there. No, it was something like night. None of the buildings had lights on. However, something dark and oppressive lay on the town, something unnatural. This was the other sort of darkness. The sort she'd always denied the existence of, as a vicar, and didn't quite believe the hype of now. The darkness that gave the word "dark" a bad name. Because all sorts of things that were dark, including the night, including people, were natural and good.

"Good afternoon," said David Cummings, stepping out of nowhere to stand beside her.

Zoya Boyko lived at 19 John Whittingham Road, which landlord Mitch said he'd got cheap, because of the address. Zoya shared his pain. She was sure she only got half of her mail. She was always missing official letters about Jas. She'd only learned about this problem from the neighbours after she'd moved in. John Whittingham Road had been named after a beloved town mayor. Except the county council had got his name wrong. It was actually "Wittingham" without the first "h." But by the time John Wittingham himself had noticed and complained, the signs had gone up, the budget spent. So John Whittingham Road, spelled wrong, had become a thing. But the county council had then felt that this might be a bad look for them come election time, or that was how the neighbours had put it, so when the next phase of building had started, a few months later, the council had had another ceremony, in an entirely different location, and had unveiled John Wittingham Road, correctly spelled. John Wittingham Road was placed on the other side of town from John Whittingham Road, which the county council had probably thought would help avoid confusion, but that meant in practice that visitors who'd picked the wrong one still had quite a walk ahead of them and that post office and delivery people didn't hedge their bets and try both addresses. The post office in the marketplace had special pigeonholes set aside for all those affected, including one for Zoya and one for those who lived at the other address. Zoya was always saying she should go and talk to whoever that was, but had never had the time to do so. To add insult to injury, even the postcodes were only one digit apart.

This was where Zoya had found herself in England, in a deluded town in a flat she couldn't afford in a street named after nobody. Now she went quickly inside, changed out of her work uniform, and left again in the direction of the school. The streets were still remarkably deserted. She'd taken a look on her phone at the town's Facebook group. Everyone was so scared of "them" who were "coming." Just the same as always, then, for English people. This lot must think all their worst tabloid fears were coming true.

As she passed one house, she saw a curtain twitching violently. The old lady inside was gesturing at her to get indoors.

Zoya waved back. "Hello, mad granny!" She wanted to call something rather ruder, but this had been a nice impulse on the part of the lady, deluded as she was. However, Zoya was not going to be lured into shared cuckoo land. She was going to get her daughter, thank you very much.

What did her mother's books say about situations like this? They were odd books, full of wisdom, a sort of philosophical system that Zoya hadn't even begun to categorise. Ah yes. "You will see the line to your objective. You will read the map when others are lost in it. You will end up where you need to be."

Well, that sort of applied. So many things in those books sort of applied. Lychford had, just sometimes, when she'd had a few moments to go and walk in the woods, felt like where she was supposed to be. Then the love she'd felt so distantly seemed to make sense. The trouble was, it had this awkward, conflicted, angular modern British town on top of it, getting in the way.

Zoya saw several other curtains twitching as she marched past. She ignored them as she always had.

Lizzie had managed to control her breathing and had turned to look at David Cummings. This "man" was a supernatural being of some kind, who she'd initially encountered when she'd first got involved with Autumn's shop. He'd been posing then as the representative of a supermarket chain. He still wore the same business suit. Back then, Lizzie had denied him his victory and exiled him from her church by burning an enormous sum of money, something that, now the whole town knew about magic, Lizzie had been absurdly worried about her treasurer discovering.

"I've got nothing to say to you," she said. She was sure he was here, wherever this was, to interrogate her. Or if this was hell, then he was here as the thing she least wanted to meet. If he did ask questions, she decided, she wasn't going to answer with anything useful. That attitude might give her a shot at not quite revealing how terrified she was of him.

"I'm quite surprised to see you up and about," he said. Which not only ignored what she'd said but made no sense. "Why are you awake?"

"Am I . . . not meant to be?" And now she'd engaged with him, damn it.

"I suppose you're the first human we've tried this on." He took a few steps nearer to the vision of Lychford and seemed to peer down into it. "Wow. You're out cold down there instead. Not what we expected at all. Still, this is fine. We've got you here, at least."

"Where is this?"

"Do you like it?" Cummings gestured around him. "All my own work. They say the sign of something is the thing itself. But that's a human idea that's crept into magic. A lot of the people on my side don't credit stuff like that. They don't like to think we've been polluted by you. But we have been. That will all be over soon, though, of course."

"Not going to happen." Could she feel her usual sense of the presence of God in the world, even here? She wasn't sure. It was the most subtle of flavours at the best of times.

"I mention that because this place is definitely the sign of something. But it's easy to see that it isn't a thing itself. I made it to look like nothing much at all. Deliberately. Because fuck all these worlds of yours with all their fucking clutter."

"Charming as ever. You still talk like you own the place."

"In this case, I really do."

"But I always had the feeling you were the monkey, not the organ grinder."

"Oh, I've ground a few organs. Nothing? Not even a little smile? Come on, it wouldn't kill you, would it?"

"You tell me." She had the wonderful feeling she was actually getting under his skin, by the simple method of treating everything he said like a trap. Or was that sense of power on her part the actual trap? Was he hoping that she'd get overconfident and start talking? What did she even have to reveal?

He stepped closer to her and reached out to put his hand on her face. She did her best not to flinch. It felt exactly like a human hand. "Disruption is the most important thing. You take the rules, and you rip them up, and in ripping them up, you show everyone that the so-called rules are just polite conventions, just manners. After you rip them up you can create your own manners, your own rules. If you want to."

"You really took onboard what you heard at all those human business seminars. What would stop anyone else ripping those new rules up? How is this not just a chain reaction of . . . wrongness?"

"Oh, you would think it's wrong. It's your reality we're about to rip up."

"Nope."

"What do you mean 'nope'?"

Lizzie had thought of something to say that might get him to reveal even more about what was going on. "I'm safe at home in bed. This isn't real. It's just a nightmare."

He slapped her across the face.

The blow was so hard she fell to the ground. Before she could even cry out, he'd stepped forward to stand above her, shouting. "No, you are not fucking dreaming! This is more real than anything you have experienced in your pitiful life, you fucking deluded cow!"

Lizzie slowly hauled herself back on to her feet. She made herself say words through her bruised lips. "I'm not afraid of you. You can get behind me."

"I'm only a representative, not the boss. But my boss isn't Satan. Or he only is because you all said he was."

"Really?" Lizzie tried hard to sound like she didn't believe him.

"Millions of years ago, he made a mistake, that's all. He tried to work with the underpinnings of all existence.

And it's not like there was a higher authority to judge him, as your tales say, because of course you've all heard about this and jumped to the wrong conclusions. This was just an accident. But what he did... created this extra world—this extra universe, to use your word for it—which you all came to inhabit."

Lizzie didn't, of course, believe the creation stories of the Bible to be the literal truth. She did, however, believe that God had been responsible for the creation of the universe, probably through all the fine detail that Professor Brian Cox liked to describe on TV. "They used to give Lucifer credit for giving humanity knowledge or fire. Now he's bigged himself up to the point of creating the universe. When what you're actually talking about is the Fall."

"Reality is nothing like your stories."

"Would your boss even know, seriously, if there was anyone above him? Or does he know there is, and is still scared of the managing director? Hence all the lies."

Cummings seemed to decide to ignore this new tack of hers entirely. Which Lizzie found both indicative and pleasing. "We of all the original worlds, all of whom knew of each other, all of whom had been mucking along together without any big bangs or anything like that, forever, were quite surprised, following the boss's *accident*, that now there was an extra world, with a weird new sort of time in it that we couldn't really get our heads around. But okay, we thought, more stuff, great. However, by the time we started to colonise the place, there *you* all were, *evolving*, with your *science,* and all your other shitty ideas."

"Still not nodding along. But do go on."

"And by the time we'd got our heads around that, because of this weird time of yours, you were full-on established and had made pets of the fairies, and then you suddenly had nuclear weapons and plagues and stuff and woah, the boss woke up from where he lies underneath all things and started thinking it was time to tidy up this error, to reel it all back into the mainstream. Hence today."

"What?"

"You're all going to finally meet the big man from head office. And you'll find he's terribly persuasive."

———————

Autumn had decanted the blue liquid from the arrows into several beakers and was now trying to work out what she could do to test it. Damn it, she was only just starting to learn how to apply science to this stuff. This was a poison, right? So it had to be biologically active. So how did you test that? She had no internet to look it up on.

As she was stirring one of the beakers, trying to think, something also stirred in her coat pocket. Her extra senses were feeling something. She took out the thing wrapped in newspaper that Judith had sent to Sunil. She could see it pulsing. It wasn't just emanating the potential for life now but also . . . need. She held it closer to the beaker. The need increased. If it could move, it would have moved toward the liquid that had been shot into Lizzie.

That was weird. Why did this thing want poison? Was it part of some evil creature? Why would Judith have given that to Sunil? Why would she have given *anything* magical to Sunil, rather than to them?

She had nothing else to work with. She didn't want to cut this thing up, in case integrity was important for whatever it did. She took a dripper, sucked up a tiny sample of the liquid, and dripped it on the organ. The flesh visibly grew newer, more like something that should be inside a living body. This . . . poison . . . was feeding whatever this was. Like this was the blood it was used to being supplied with.

Why would an enemy try to inject them with another creature's blood?

Okay, all in or not?

She decided. She poured the whole beaker over the organ, then grabbed another one. The meat started to pulse with life. She could actually see it growing now. She emptied the next beaker. She only had three left. Should she use them? What was it growing into?

To her amazement, as she watched, the organ started to grow vestigial arms . . . and then a head. Oh God, this was all getting a bit John Carpenter.

Which was when the shop bell rang, urgently, insistently, as if the person ringing it was being chased by something.

And she'd left Lizzie in the shop, on two chairs shoved together, covered by a blanket.

She put down the remaining beakers and ran to the door.

She immediately saw that outside stood Luke. She let him in.

"What's going on?" he said. "Are you all right?" Then he looked to where Lizzie lay, and his expression grew even more concerned. "Shit. Is she okay?"

So she told him the details of what he'd heard already as garbled rumour. As she did so, she became aware of a sound coming from the back room. A sort of . . . mewling. "Oh dear," she said.

"You've got . . . something in there, right? Again." He'd put a hand over his crotch, Autumn realised, obviously remembering what had happened last time. He saw her looking and moved it away again. "If so, I'm once again here to put my groin between you and danger."

"Let's hope it doesn't come to that," said Autumn. She went to the inner door and hesitantly opened it. Luke, even more hesitantly, followed.

Something was lying on the table, something that looked vaguely like a human body. As Autumn and Luke watched, it reached out a thin, half-formed bundle of spindly fingers, grabbed the next beaker full of blue liquid, and sat up to drink it. Shape and form pulsed into its body as it did so. It was becoming, every moment, more and more of an adult male. It was looking at them curiously. Not, thankfully, with any aggression. It seemed to be thriving on the very stuff that Autumn had been thinking of as a poison.

Luke put a hand on Autumn's shoulder. "Did you . . . make him?"

Before Autumn could answer, the creature raised a thin finger and pointed it, shaking, toward Luke. "Daddy," it said.

Autumn couldn't help but raise an eyebrow at her boyfriend. "Did *you*?"

Lizzie had allowed Cummings to lead her to where they could see the vision of Lychford in more detail. She got the feeling she was looking at the equivalent of a tactical map, because in whichever direction she looked, the view obligingly opened up to her extra senses to show whatever was around the corner. It was like a magical Google Street View. It was also, now she could see close up, full of a jumbled mass of letters and numbers, in which she could pick out the odd familiar address. She could see people moving around in the map, too, but they were jumbled masses of information that changed every moment. Elements of who they were were suddenly deemed to be important by the map and leapt out: post sender . . . oh, that person was in the post office. That was how rough the underlying data was. This visual assault of alphabets and number systems must be how magical beings from other realms saw human civilisation, much as Cummings had described it. This display spoke of an attempt to make sense of that jumble. Individual addresses and house names would loom out of it when she turned her attention to them. So this was a very awkward first attempt at getting to grips with the territory Cummings's side were preparing to attack. Cummings himself must see things more clearly than this, surely? But perhaps that was only when he was in her world. So was this weird world where she'd woken up the headquarters of Cummings's boss? No. Surely he wouldn't have brought her there? She tried moving from side to side a little and confirmed what she'd just noticed: there seemed to be a slight disconnect between the view of Lychford and the world where they stood, a gap between the two. "How do I get back home?" she asked, hoping that would sound despairing enough to seem like a real question. Actually, she was hoping he'd tell her more about this display.

"You can't get there from here. No more than you could leap into a television and visit Coronation Street. I've only put this here for my own convenience, so I can keep track of what's going on."

Ah. That was it. So perhaps the boss, wherever he was, was looking at a bigger version. Lizzie could feel with her extra senses that the vision in front of her was, in some sense, the real Lychford, that what she was seeing were real people in real time. What else could she feel around here? It wasn't all dull emptiness, was it? Not quite. There was something a way off behind her. It reminded her of . . . what she'd felt on the few occasions she'd been close to the border of the land of fairy. She let her extra senses have a bit of a wander back there. She felt . . . oh. She turned and looked but couldn't see anything. "Who's out there?" Again, she hoped she sounded scared. That hardly required method acting.

Cummings grinned horribly. "Who do you think it is?"

"Fairies. There are lots of fairies here. Only . . ."

"Yes?"

"They're very quiet. Not *entirely* here."

She looked back to him. He was still smiling. Like he was a quiz show host and she'd just got a correct answer. There was a stillness about what was behind her. That was what she'd felt. If there were fairies here, they didn't glow with possibility and wonder and scariness like the genuine fairy country on the horizon had, like those fairy warriors that had once threatened her and those lost ravers. It was the same sensation but . . . asleep. Like her own body was supposed to be. While her mind was here. "Your games are pretty meaningless," said Cummings. "Escape being conceptually impossible, so—"

Lizzie didn't hear the end of his sentence. She was already running toward the fairies.

"Daddy . . . sorry, Dad, Father . . ." The being was slowly getting off the table.

Autumn couldn't help but wonder if its nakedness was leading to Luke making unfortunate comparisons. "It's not a contest," she said to him, without quite meaning to.

"What?"

"Nothing."

"Does he need help?"

"Nothing we could give him," said Autumn. Luke was, she realised, seeing his first fairy. Because her extra senses were now yelling at her that that was what had formed out of the lump that Judith had left for Sunil.

"Greetings," said Luke, going over to awkwardly address the mass of growing flesh. "We are friendly."

"Thanks," said the fairy. "Me too."

"Excuse me for asking," said Autumn, "but why do you think he's your father?"

"Sorry." The slowly forming being said. "Imp . . . imprinting? Is that a word? We just . . . sop up whatever influences are around us when we're in this state, and I'm not used to being born in the . . . human world, is it? Charming as ever! Small but lovely! Ah, I have a name of my own, there it is. I'm—" He made a long, complicated whistling sound, like a flute doing a particularly complex piece of classical music.

"Terrific," said Autumn. "Easy to shout in dangerous situations. I'm going to call you Trill."

"Like the bird seed," said Luke. "A novelty name. We are terrible parents."

"So that'll be my name here," said Trill. "Thanks for sorting that, Mum."

"Please could you stop that?"

"*He* said 'parents,'" said Trill, indicating Luke. "That

took my imprinting to maximum."

His accent, Autumn realised, and his speech habits, sounded quite a lot like Luke. "Do you know what you are, Trill?"

"I'm a fairy. In the service of King so-and-so whose name I'm not even going to bother trying to adapt to your senses, because I think I might be offended by what you'd boil it down to."

"Would that be the same king who's the father of Finn?"

"Finn? Oh. Yes, that's the name the prince took when he came here."

Autumn wondered what long-ago encounter had caused Finn to take that name and sound Irish. But there was no time for that now. "What was that you grew from? Was that your heart?"

"Might well have been. Thanks for that." He started to experimentally walk around the room. "The last thing I remember . . . I was in a storm. At the edge of the woods. There was lightning. Oh. I know. A tree fell on me. Right at the border with the human world. I'd just been to visit a lovely English girl."

"Maybe some clothes?" suggested Luke.

"Oh, thank you."

Luke's expression said that he hadn't expected to be the one to actually provide them, but now the thought had occurred he nodded. "I'll see what I can find." And he went to head upstairs.

"So," said Autumn, "you don't remember how you came to be just a heart?"

"No. But it must be thanks to someone who really knows how my people work. A great deal of magic would be required to save my essence before I popped my clogs."

"It might have been my friend Judith who saved you."

"If you say so. I gather she's not here for me to thank?"

"No. Oh." Autumn had had a sudden, hopeful thought. She went to a cupboard, opened it, and produced Finn's head. "Could you perhaps help me with this?"

Trill yelled and leapt back a few feet. "What the hell? Why have you got the prince's head in a . . . cupboard?"

"I didn't hurt him! I just . . . put him in . . . I've been trying to heal him, okay?"

Trill was now fully formed and not at all gooey anymore and really very naked. He performatively took a deep breath and went to take the head from Autumn. He stopped, obviously realising something. "Oh, this was deliberately done to the prince. Someone wanted to stop him from being healed. I'd heard about it in old stories, but never seen it done. It would take great power to make him grow again. More than it took to keep me safe in the form of a heart."

"But it is possible to heal him?"

"Maybe. Who did this?"

Autumn did her best to get him up to speed with what they knew about the situation, trying not to look directly at him, or his bits, as she did. He looked pained to hear about it. "Who . . . who would oppose the king?"

"If your world is anything like ours, there are a lot of people who'd oppose any sort of inherited monarchical system with a built-in power imbalance."

"What?"

"Sorry," said Autumn, "just saying."

"Our system isn't like that. You just think it is because you lot copied it off us and filled it up with loads of your own nonsense and basically got it wrong."

"Oh, because usually I hear it's you who copy us."

"Over the millennia there's been a *lot* of cultural exchange. Both ways. Our king is formed from, influenced by, *all* our . . . wishes, our desires. He's an individual fairy, yes, one who's found at birth, but one who, through his blood, creates and broadcasts a consensus of what our society is. He's the collective spirit of the fairies."

"So fairyland is sort of a democracy?"

Trill sighed. "You're still trying to pin your words on us."

"I note it's a king rather than a queen."

"I suppose most fairies wanted a father."

"And now we're in the comments section."

"There may be some inequalities built into the system. Maybe you caught that from us, maybe the other way around. Mistakes were made. This is literally the first time I've thought about this."

"Definitely the comments section." But Autumn decided it was time she let him off the hook, before he decided, in the way fairies often seemed to, that he didn't owe her any more favours. She took the head back from him, and, more gently than she perhaps would have in other circumstances, returned it to the cupboard. "This accident of yours. What year was ... ?" She stopped herself, remembering that fairies didn't have much time for human calendars. "The human world when you visited, what was it like? If Judith saved you, it could be any time in the last few decades."

"It had changed a lot since the previous time I'd been here. There were lorries, bicycles, CD players ..."

"Can you remember anything from pop culture? Did this girl you were seeing like any music?"

"Yeah. Something awful. What was it? Oh ..." Trill tried whistling a few bars of what Autumn swiftly recognised as "Wonderwall" by Oasis.

"So Judith found you, changed you, saved you, and kept your heart all that time without reviving you. And then she left it to someone else rather than us. Any idea why?"

"To revive me, you'd need a supply of fairy blood. And she might not have known that's what you needed. I mean, that's sort of a secret for us? About the rest, no idea."

"So that blue stuff was fairy blood? You're literally blue-blooded?" Autumn was thinking quickly. "Is it poison to humans?"

"What? Of course not. We've taken on physical aspects of you as well. We couldn't mate with you and have kids if we were poison, could we?"

"What are we talking about?" said Luke, coming back in, carrying clothes.

"Lizzie," said Autumn. She looked back to Trill. "Our friend got shot with the same stuff you used to revive yourself. You're sure it's your everyday fairy blood, that it's not poisoned for you as well?"

"I'm fine. That's all I know." He took the clothes from Luke and started putting them on.

"So why did it make Lizzie sick?"

"It shouldn't. It should make her feel pretty damn excellent."

"Can you do anything to help her?"

Trill nodded. "I can try. That'll make us even. And then I should go home and fight for the king. Until that gets dull."

————

Lizzie sprinted through the void, making herself not care about falling, wondering every moment if the structure of this world was such that David Cummings could just have it rear up and grab her. But no, this place didn't feel random like that. It felt organised. Like one of her spreadsheets. Over there was Google Lychford, and this place itself was . . . a storage facility of some kind. Maybe it was just like all the other realities that bordered Lychford, that had existed, according to Cummings, forever, except this one was entered by minds rather than bodies. A sort of dreamland. A tamed and organised one. It certainly felt like she was getting somewhere, not like in one of those dreams where your feet are in treacle. But it was very Cummings to allow her hope in order to dash it away. So Lizzie was keeping all her faith and hope locked inside her.

She was running toward that low, dull feeling of fairies. As she ran, that feeling resolved itself into lots of individual sources. They were just . . . standing here. And then she could see them. Ahead of her were appearing rows of silent, immobile fairies, warriors and workers, men, women, and children, all of them staring into space, their arms by their sides, as if expecting something that wasn't arriving. Lizzie slowed to walk through their ranks. There were hundreds of them here, maybe thousands. Row upon row of them went back into the darkness, beyond where she could see. Here was one with a lovely brooch pinning his cloak, here was another with jewellery in her hair that looked too fine to have been spun by human hands. They each still felt unearthly. All of them hit the uncanny valley full on, felt beyond human while toying with the idea of being human. Except that sounded artificial when her experience of fairies was that they somehow felt more authentic than humans did. She wanted to try to wake them, but with the depth of the sleep she could feel here, she knew that would be impossible. Also, frankly, she was scared to. Behind them, further back, she could feel a much bigger source of the same feeling, all concentrated in one place, one body. And with it there was also . . . yeah, there it was, enormous terror. The sort of fear that Autumn had described concerning her own first journey into the land of fairy.

That would be Finn's father. That would be their king.

———————

Autumn led the newly clothed Trill into the shop area, where Lizzie lay. The fairy was now dressed in Autumn's own spare pyjamas, Wellington boots, and a jumper of Luke's that he'd left in her bedroom. Autumn couldn't sense the assailants nearby, so maybe she really had banished them from this world, but that didn't mean there weren't others. It occurred to her that she'd just discovered one way of getting past the barrier, but it didn't feel like one where a human would survive the trip. "Hey," she said to Trill as he bent to examine Lizzie, "do you know where other fairies are? I mean, can you sense them?"

"Like fae-dar," suggested Luke.

"I can when we're against the background of this world." Trill seemed to consider, then stood up and turned like a weathervane, pointing. "There are two of them about nine hundred strides away. They feel . . . asleep. They're heading toward where you used to keep all the . . . magnet . . . stuff, but now it's all moved?"

It took Autumn a while and a few more questions to understand that he was talking about "north," magnetic north having once, in the memory of Trill's people, approximated to compass north, but now being something more like northwest. What was north of here? Nothing special that she could think of. The "asleep" bit seemed to square with how she'd felt about the assassins. Nine hundred strides, that was . . . actually quite a long way. "Okay, putting that aside for now, what can you do to help my friend?"

Trill frowned. "I can feel the fairy blood in her. It feels

weird. Different. But I don't know why it's hurting her. It must have been . . . changed somehow, infected."

"But you re-grew yourself using that blood," said Autumn. "Wouldn't it have poisoned you too?"

"I'm sure it would," said Trill. "But I feel fine."

"And if the idea is to poison you two with arrows," said Luke, "why not just use actual poison rather than altered blood?"

"No idea. But you know, this stuff is a vital part of all fairies, our connection to the king." He seemed puzzled by the lack of reaction on their part. "I mean, I can just take it back."

They both turned to look at him at once.

———————

David Cummings once again appeared beside Lizzie, making her jump. "You're wondering why you're not staring into space like they are," he said, continuing the conversation as if no running away had been involved. "So am I. I think it must be because you're human and they're not."

Lizzie took a couple of steps further along the rows of motionless fairies. "Is there that much difference between us?"

"We're trying to keep part of the fairy minds conscious, the part that's running the belief system we've infected them with, so their bodies can work for us. The reasoning part of them is here, the part that responds to personally adapted and endlessly morphing fantasies about freedom and eternal justice is out there in their physical brains. The boss can issue specific commands through the king, but our good fairies are perfectly capable of carrying out the mission without us micromanaging. Human minds are weaker, so you just got knocked out and came here entirely. Note to self: we'll need to use a smaller dose on the rest of you."

"A smaller dose of what?"

"Fairy blood. As produced by the king. We started out by infecting just a few fairies, whom we'd persuaded to listen to our point of view. They began the civil war in fairy. They infected more and more to their side, which was secretly our side by proxy, until we managed to land a blood arrow on the king, and then, bingo, he broadcasts the infection to the rest, war's over, we won. A few of the stronger-willed fairies held out, like the prince, Finn. So we hunted those down and finished them off."

Lizzie hoped her expression conveyed the disgust and anger she felt. "I know."

"Oh, do you think we're bullying the fairies?" Cummings pointed to the comatose examples around them.

"These people, if they can be called that, are by their very nature traitors. They want somebody to love. As I said, they've always been soft on humans. As soon as that extra universe sprouted, fairies settled this world, but when you people arrived, they took one look at you and, well, I'd say 'went native' but they *were* the natives. It was Stockholm syndrome, I suppose. They came to identify with their oppressors. Which is a hilarious name for that condition, because let me tell you, the magical races of Stockholm don't feel that way at all."

"And neither do your people?"

"Correct."

"Possibly because we exist because of a mistake made by your boss? Do you feel we're your mess to clean up?"

She was pleased and scared to see she'd made him angry again. "It's more about the persecution. Those of us who'd been used to roaming freely around this new world, those of us who didn't want to become your lap dogs, we found ourselves cast in the role of devils and evil spirits and whatever your current dominant religious paradigm thought was icky. Even the fairies could never quite be submissive enough to earn your trust."

"Most people these days don't think *any* of you are real."

"Oh, of course, you've forgotten, and that makes it all right. You're not responsible for what your ancestors did. That's what they all say. Most of the time for us it has indeed been a choice between evil and imaginary. There have always been exceptions, humans who thought we were charming, dangerously attractive, forbidden. They've often been useful idiots for us. And from time to time, before the boss woke up, I can't deny it, our leaders have negotiated, hence the handful of agreements that led to some of the borders around Lychford. Most of those borders, however, were forced on our worlds, shutting us off in our . . . reservations. But we've been watching from them, learning about all your little cultural vulnerabilities. Now, across the realms, there's a consensus, led by the boss now naptime is over. Your world is going to embrace reality. Become again part of *our* realities. By force."

Lizzie was sure this was the same manifesto that Maitland Picton had talked about. Picton's plan had been to pull the whole of the human world into the other realms at once. But Lizzie and Autumn had got the feeling that she was something of a rogue agent, completing her assigned mission, but in her own way. Still, despite being scared of Cummings, as well as deeply annoyed by him, Lizzie felt there was something she should say at this point. Because he had to hear this from at least one human. "Listen," she said. "I agree about the historical wrongs done to your people."

"Oh! Thank you so much! That makes it all so much better! There's a 'but' coming up, though, isn't there? As in 'but we'd like to keep all the land we shut you out of, please.'"

"I agree we've done wrong. I want us to recognise that. I want us to do something about it. And I want you to remember that."

"That's the most passive-aggressive threat I've ever heard. From a position of no strength at all. What, you think the cavalry is coming?"

Lizzie made herself straighten up and look him in the eye. Accepting the truth about her own side gave her the strength to do that. "I *know* they are."

3

ZOYA HAD ARRIVED AT the school gate, set in a low wall and still with its usual padlock. Visitors during the day couldn't access the playground, they had to go around to the office. The school looked deserted. Where the hell was Jas? Now was not the time for niceties. She jogged up to the gate and vaulted it, then walked quickly over to the school buildings. "Hello?" she called. She could see movement inside. She went up to one of the classroom doors and it was quickly opened.

Charlie, Jas's teaching assistant, leapt out, grabbed her, and pulled her in. "Quickly!"

Inside, Zoya found a bunch of adults, teachers, teaching assistants, and even school dinner ladies, hunkered down behind upturned tables. They were clutching various implements, from carving knives to hammers, and they looked very determined. "Oh," she sighed. "They shall not pass. Whoever they are."

"You have to get down," said Charlie, trying to lead her into cover. But Zoya shook off her grasp.

"Where's Jas?"

"With the other children. Mrs. Williams has them in the main hall, behind some improvised defences. It's in the middle of the building. We thought it'd be safest."

"What do you think you're doing? What are you defending them from? You're scaring them with all this rubbish."

Mrs. Cotton, the deputy head, poked her head up from behind one of the tables. She was wearing a teacher's expression so fierce that Zoya immediately wanted to say she was sorry and wouldn't do it again, whatever it was. "We have intruders on the grounds. Very strange intruders. Several members of staff have seen them. 999 doesn't work. Shaun Mawson is on his way over. I assure you this is real. And you're right, they shall not pass. Not while we have anything to say about it. Now get under cover."

Zoya folded her arms, a little perturbed by the woman's certainty. "I didn't see anything."

"And you can't feel it?" said Charlie. The teaching assistant put a hand to her own head. "You can't feel the . . . weird stuff that's out there right now?"

"With what, my psychic powers? What? What are you all looking at?" Zoya had suddenly become aware that all of them were looking past her to the window behind her. Their faces were pictures of shock and dismay. Okay. She'd play along.

Zoya slowly turned to see what all the fuss was about.

———————————

Autumn was watching Trill, who'd put his fingers on the artery at Lizzie's throat, a look of concentration on his face. Fairies didn't seem to need all the words, gestures, and sacrifices that humans did in order to perform magic. He'd told them that if he could feel this infected blood doing anything weird to him, he'd stop. The blue liquid pulsed in Lizzie's throat, then suddenly started to flow into the space between that throat and Trill's fingers. Her skin remained unbroken. The blood was hissing from her pores, Autumn realised, pouring from her in a mist. As Autumn watched, the colour of her friend's face started to return to normal.

———————————

Zoya couldn't see what the teachers were gawping at.

She turned and walked toward the window. "See?" she said. "Nothing." She looked back over her shoulder at them. "You're all bonkers mental."

Charlie got up with the obvious intention of trying to make her retreat, but one of the others pulled her back. "You really can't see it?" she whispered.

"No. What can you see?" Zoya turned back and put her hand up against the window. These ridiculous individuals. Still, it was weird that they were all having the same hallucination at once. Maybe some passing shadow out there had set them off? Was there anything out there at all?

"No," called Mrs. Cotton, as if to something outside the window. "Don't!"

Zoya felt something strike her. She put a hand to her chest. It was like she'd had a sudden cramp in a place she hadn't been aware it was possible to have one. Pins and needles started to radiate out from her collarbone. Her mum had had a word for when you got a sudden ache you couldn't account for, she remembered. She'd called it being "fairy struck." She waved her hand in front of her. Was she touching something? Was there something sticking in her? She couldn't see it. She could barely feel it. And yet . . . and yet she was feeling . . . very weird.

She turned back to the classroom and pointed at the teachers angrily. "What is this fu—?"

And then the darkness rushed into her head and she fell.

———

"Understand this, you hypocritical sack of shit, we're going to be rid of you!" Cummings was shouting, advancing on Lizzie. She was slowly backing away, but now she was cornered against the front row of entranced fairies. She fell and he loomed over her, filling her vision with his snarling features. "Oh, are you thinking about running, maybe going to find the fairy king? Please do. The boss is right there with him. He'd barely notice you as his presence extinguished you. No, we're finally going to be rid of all of you. And *nobody* is coming to save—"

He suddenly stopped, an odd look on his face. There had, Lizzie realised, been a sound, a thump, like a piece of wood hitting something.

Cummings fell aside, his eyes closing as he hit the forest floor, unconscious.

Behind him stood a young woman with very short hair and very loud makeup. She held in her hands a sturdy piece of wood. "As I was saying," she yelled, in what sounded like a Russian accent, "what is this fuckwittery?" She seemed to reconsider in the moment as she saw Lizzie's clerical collar. "Reverend?"

Lizzie opened her mouth to answer. But she realised that she was feeling weird again. She started to form some sort of reply, but then—

She woke up again.

And she was back in Autumn's shop and staring up at Autumn.

Oh God. She had so much to say. "Thank you. You brought me back."

"Any time," said Autumn. "*Every* time."

Lizzie had to bite her lip. She wanted to say more, but actually there was Luke, and . . . also a fairy in pyjamas and wellies. "Shit," she said. "I'm still dreaming."

"No," said Autumn, "he's real. I have a lot to tell you."

Lizzie sat up. "*I* have a lot to tell *you,* and you need to hear mine first. Yes, you do. No, shut up. Does anyone here know any Russians?"

And now Autumn was looking at her like she was mad. But then Autumn's phone beeped with an incoming text. She looked at the screen. "The school say they've just had a fairy attack. With a . . . Ukrainian victim. Could that be—?"

"Oh," said Lizzie. "Can we not tell her I thought she was Russian?"

————————

Autumn quickly packed a bag with everything she could think of that might help, while she, Luke, and Trill listened to Lizzie explain that David Cummings seemed to have the fairies and their king asleep in a dream world and was controlling their bodies here through infected fairy blood.

Trill told her to stop, concentrated for a moment, then nodded, looking angry. "I can't feel the presence of the king," he said. "Not at all. Not like he's dreaming. Nothing. What's that about? Is that to do with why I'm not being controlled like these others?"

"No idea," said Autumn. "We need more information."

"We will have revenge," said the fairy. "How dare another nation meddle in our affairs, to the point of leading us?"

"You're sounding less like me all the time," noted Luke.

"They grow up so quickly," said Autumn.

"That's the mistake people make," said Trill. "People and demons too. We enjoy being influenced. Just like humans do. But we are actually strong enough to assert ourselves."

"Unlike humans," said Autumn.

"Not all humans," said Luke.

"Influence and belief," continued Trill, "are the underpinnings of all the worlds, all the realities, as you'd say. Except perhaps this one, which has this physics thing, which I agree is a terrible idea, if I may say so."

"That's fascinating," said Autumn. "After this is over, I want to hear all about that, with my notebooks handy. And probably a stiff drink. But. Moving on."

Lizzie finished her story, taking it up to the moment

of the satisfying impact of wood on demon skull. "What does that woman knocking Cummings out even mean?" she said. "He was surprised I was awake, so I guess humans could do things in that dream world he didn't expect. Though I don't think he was lying about how impossible it would be to help the king. But is that woman's mind safe there when Cummings wakes up? What does 'waking up' there involve?"

"Let's see if we can get her out of there before he does." Autumn grabbed her keys and led them out of the door. She hoped her gait looked much more confident than she was feeling.

———

As the clock in the church tower struck noon, Autumn and her party marched toward the school. They could move with reasonable speed, given that Trill would be able to warn them of approaching fairies. But it occurred to Autumn that that was a two-edged sword. "If you can sense them, they can sense you," she said.

Trill looked uncertain. "I'm not so sure. I'm not getting any response back from them. I feel rather like I've put a glamour on myself, like I'm invisible."

"Also," said Lizzie, "if they're using that map I saw to navigate through the town, they'll be a bit all over the place. If 'post sender' was what leapt out from the post office, that's like they're getting vague thoughts from people here and using them to navigate. 'Post' wouldn't mean anything to fairies." She looked to Trill. "Would it?"

"Only so many people need posts," said the fairy, "and where do they need to be sent?"

"My case rests," said Lizzie.

Autumn was pleased that they were once again working together pretty well. But it worried her that they still hadn't got to the heart of what the problem had been in the first place. Lizzie now seemed to be displaying a slightly exaggerated niceness to Luke, as if she was making up for an issue she still felt but didn't want to express. But later for all that. (She hoped there would *be* a later for all that.) "Anyway," she said, "if Trill senses a fairy nearby, and if they start moving toward us, we head in the other direction. Okay?"

It took them another ten minutes to get to the end of the footpath that connected to the main road going past the school. "They must be able to come and go through this barrier themselves," said Lizzie. "They wouldn't have set up a wall the rest of their forces couldn't pass through."

"But why have a wall at all?" said Autumn. "Doesn't an invading army want people to run away and let them have the territory?"

"They're not invading," said Lizzie. "That Picton woman talked about transforming the world, making it into a land like the magic one she came from. And Cummings's boss seems to have similar plans. Cummings said they were going to rip up our reality."

As they approached the school, they slowed down, but Trill shook his head. "There aren't any fairies nearby. They've gone."

"What were they after?" wondered Autumn as they climbed over the locked gate into the deserted playground. From the texts she was getting from inside the building, there had been only the one casualty, this Ukrainian woman. She texted back to tell the teachers that the enemy had departed.

"Oh," said Luke, the sound of realisation in his voice. "It's about you."

"What?" said Lizzie.

"These are commando attacks against individual targets. What? I read a lot of military history. They weren't here to storm the school or terrorise it, they were just here to take out this Ukrainian woman. Mission accomplished, so then they left. But before coming here, they tried to take out you two."

"And there was another target," said Trill, "they went toward this 'not about magnets any more' direction thing of yours first, and this is not that."

"So I reckon that's what the wall is for, to stop you two getting away. Maybe this woman here too. The three of you, plus maybe this other target to the north, must be the ones who can stop whatever huge transforming magical shit they're planning."

"Oh my God," said Autumn, flattered and terrified at once. She could see the same emotions on Lizzie's face too.

"Don't sound so surprised," said Luke. "You're pretty awesome."

"So how is the Ukrainian awesome?" said Autumn.

"Awesome enough to thump Cummings around the head in dreamland," said Lizzie.

———————

The teachers thankfully let them inside, and they found the young woman with the short hair whom Lizzie recognised from the dream world still unconscious and being kept warm in the staff room. "Do you want me to do the thing again?" asked Trill.

They watched as he drained the fairy blood from the young woman's body. The teachers looked on in awe, although they were at the same time taking turns to make cups of hot soup. From the noise further inside the building, it became clear that a general evacuation of children had started. "We were telling parents to stay away," said Mrs. Cotton, "but now they're arriving to take the children home. We've got a lot of couples where one of them was caught outside this wall thing. They must be worried sick."

Lizzie just nodded. She was very much feeling the responsibility now. Especially if this was all about the two . . . or three . . . of them.

"So you're going to do something about this, right?" That was another teacher, a thin man with a beard. "I mean, we don't deserve this. It has to stop."

"Go and see to the evacuation, please, Mr. Moore," said Mrs Cotton. After a moment's hesitation, the man seemed to see the steel in the deputy head's eyes and left. "You've met a few like that, I should think," she said to Lizzie.

"Thank you," said Lizzie.

The young woman, who they'd been told was called Zoya, coughed, opened her eyes, and immediately sat up. "Where's Jas?"

Mrs. Cotton told her she was safe with the other children and that Zoya could see her as soon as she wanted. Zoya nodded, closed her eyes in relief, then opened them again and pointed at Lizzie. "You. You were there. Oh fucksticks. All this bollocks is true, isn't it?"

"Depending on which bollocks, but yes, probably,"

said Lizzie. "What happened after I left?"

"I looked around. Rows of . . . those guys," she said, pointing at Trill, startled all over again.

Trill waved.

"It was like the auditions for bloody *Lord of the Rings*. But no pyjamas. Then I heard that guy who was yelling at you start making little waking up noises, so I found the bit of wood and hit him again. I had to do that three more times. I got bored. I looked at my phone, but it was just a sort of prop phone, and I couldn't get any reception because I was in *Lord of the Rings,* so I'd have only got I don't know, Bugger Baggins anyway, but no, stop, just tell me what the fuck is going on!"

Which had reached a sort of panicked existential yell by the end of it. As quickly as possible, with Autumn doing most of the talking and Lizzie making the odd interjection, they provided her with a Previously On Lychford.

Zoya stared at them. "Holy shit."

"Sums it up in two words," said Lizzie.

"I was rained on too. Why don't I have these extra senses? I want my money back."

"No idea," said Autumn. "There must be some good reason why they attacked you as well as us."

"And they went north and might have attacked someone up there," added Luke.

"But nobody else appeared in the dream world," said Zoya. "Not while I was there, anyway."

"Good point," said Autumn. "If you are a target, we think it's because you might be able to hurt them, so could we please ask—?"

"No magic powers."

"Not even with the rain," said Autumn. "That is weird. But we need to make sure you're okay. Can you stick with us?"

"If I can bring Jas," said Zoya, "I'm with you ladies. But what can we do about that twat in dreamland and all these . . . bad elves?"

Lizzie realised that Autumn had been staring over at where the teachers were filling the kettle. "Where," said Autumn, "is that water coming from?"

———————

Autumn, going after a sudden new hope with the thought in her head that it might evaporate, quickly found a teacher who was in charge of the school garden, and had an allotment, and knew all about water tables and where the reservoirs were. "Nearest of those," he said, "is over in Faringdon. We're connected to the mains running down from there. Nothing to do with the river."

"So," said Autumn, feeling very pleased with herself.

"We're not actually trapped."

"Why?" asked Luke.

"Because the wall hasn't cut off the pipes underground. So it's a dome, not a sphere. So if I dig down . . . and I'm guessing the water pipes need maintenance, so they can't be very deep . . ."

"Do you mean we can get everyone out?"

This was going to be the hard bit. "No. When he wakes up, and I think we should assume he already has, Cummings would notice. His surveillance isn't great, judging by what Lizzie saw, but it's good enough to see that. He'd get his boss to send the archers to fire at the escapees. Because yeah, part of his plan does seem about taking the three of us out, but he also seems to want to keep everyone else here. I'm talking about one person sneaking out. Me."

"And going where?" asked Lizzie.

Autumn pointed at Trill. "You told us your king was the heart and soul of fairies." She pointed at Lizzie. "You felt the king was there in the dream world. But we can't get to him there. So I'm going to go into the land of fairy, find his physical form, and wake him up."

Lizzie helped the teachers get the remaining children to

their parents, though half a dozen were left with all their carers presumably outside the wall and not able to answer calls. Lizzie hoped that was the case, anyway. Those children were going to be looked after here by the staff, and presumably taken home with them at the end of the day. Lizzie had watched these wonderful people do their absolute best to keep things as normal as possible while the impossible had invaded their town. She could hear the sounds of a Pixar movie playing on a screen in the main hall. That was where Zoya had gone to find her daughter.

These people were professionals, though. And even among their number there had been some who weren't dealing, some whose idea of support was to pile pressure on herself and Autumn. What the people of Lychford thought they deserved . . . well, the extremities of that were something she'd been navigating ever since she came here. A tiny part of her was glad that the locals were going to have to deal with whatever came next. Perhaps it would bring the wisdom that she'd thought the rain would have brought. But that thought was an entirely unworthy one, born of stress and danger and . . . whatever was gnawing away at her.

Autumn had told them she was going to go to the school science lab to prepare a few things for . . . for this incredibly dangerous mission she'd decided she was going on. Now, Lizzie went to find her. She entered without knocking because if she had, Autumn would have yelled at her to go away. There was her friend, busy at the sink. Lizzie took a moment to really look at her. She was mixing some concoction, which had, as usual, put a powerful smell in the air. Only this time that smell was ... the strongest scent of coffee that Lizzie had ever encountered. And, given her own predilections, that was saying a lot. "Hey," she said.

"Hey," said Autumn, not looking round, tolerating her presence.

Lizzie went to sit on a stool. "So you're going into the land of fairy."

"Yep."

"The place that once scared you so badly it changed the course of your career and entire personality."

"I guess."

"And you're going right into the middle of it, to see the king, who was the single biggest reason for how terrifying the experience was last time."

"Lizzie, if you're just here to remind me of my fear, I don't need that, okay?" She still hadn't looked round.

"You do, because you'll face it better if you've thought about it beforehand. You know that's true." Lizzie knew where this was heading, but she couldn't help it, and the little dismissive noise Autumn made now finally set her off.

"And don't treat me like I'm an amateur who hasn't been standing right beside you as you've dealt with all this shit."

Which finally made Autumn stop and turn around. "I'm sorry," she said.

Lizzie put a hand to her own head, immediately regretting her anger. "Sorry. You saved my life. You rescued me. When I was told that was impossible. I don't have the right to—"

Autumn put down the saucepan she was holding and marched over and embraced her.

Lizzie held on for a long minute.

"What *is* it?" Autumn finally said. "What's wrong?"

"I don't know." Lizzie was being as honest as she could be. "I don't know what it is."

Autumn paused. Like she had some ideas as to what the problem might be, but didn't want to share them. "Don't you?"

"Maybe it's because you've got someone. And it's been a long time for me. And that's an awful selfish thought. I really am glad for you. And please stop saying it's because I'm worried about sex before marriage because my whole belief system is about not being judgmental, whatever a lot of my people are actually like, because we're all just stupid human beings and please don't argue with me about that right now."

"Okay." Autumn was silent again for a while. Then she

said, carefully, "You know me doing this is our only shot?"

"I don't know that. Neither do you."

"They're going to make some sort of bigger move soon. This is our move. This is our chance. I have to take it. I need to be brave. I need to do what needs to be done."

"At least let me come with you. I'm better than you at being brave."

"No you're bloody not."

"The two of us could do this better."

"Then who's going to look after the innocent by-standers when the shit goes down?"

"Damn it. I'm sorry. I'm sorry we've been . . ."

"That's over now. Probably. Or we can deal with it later. Just let me finish making this—" She meant the concoction in the beaker by the sink.

"What is it?"

"Every stimulant I can find, and I'm going to add some from the chemist on my way out of town, packed into a bottle that I've enchanted for alarm and emphasis. It's a wake-up potion for the king."

"Keep some for me when you come back."

"No."

"Just come back."

"I'll do my best."

Lizzie grabbed Autumn's face and made her look her

in the eye. "If it all goes pear-shaped, you run out of there and you get back to me. To us. You promise me."

She was suddenly on the verge of tears. And so was Autumn. "I promise."

"I lost you for too long. I was apart from you too long."

"I promise."

Lizzie was at least convinced she was going to try. She held her again. "How has Luke reacted to your plan?"

"He thinks he can persuade me not to go. Which is why I'm going to sneak out without telling him."

"No," said Lizzie, with the patience of someone who knew she was going to win an argument, "you're not."

———————

From a distance, at the end of a corridor, Lizzie watched that parting play out. Luke made big gestures with his hands. No, absolutely not. Okay, so if she was determined to go, he was going to go with her. Autumn touched him, implored him, held up her bag to show him she was prepared.

"What are they doing?" said a young voice beside Lizzie.

Lizzie looked down to see that Jas, Zoya's daughter, was standing there. "My friend Autumn is going to do something very brave," she said. "Her boyfriend doesn't want her to. He wants to come too. But that wouldn't be a good idea."

"She has to go," said Jas, as if it were the most obvious catchphrase from a beloved storybook.

Zoya poked her head out of a door, saw what was going on, and came over. "Jas, are you okay?"

"I'm okay."

Zoya looked at Lizzie. "Are *you* okay? Reverend."

Lizzie wished she'd stop calling her that. The way she said it was a barrier between them, but obviously the background she came from made her say it every time. The worst of both worlds. And she felt they'd already shared more than that. In both worlds. "Jas here was just telling me something that's true," she said. And she watched Autumn finally detach herself from Luke, look meaningfully at her for a moment, and then go on her way.

Lizzie sent all her prayers with her.

———————

Autumn met with Trill at the edge of the school playground. "Thanks," she said. "I want you to come with me down by the river, under the bridge, and up into the woods. You're my fairy assassin detector."

"And I suspect my invisibility to fairies covers those

nearby too. So I'm doubly handy. Hey, I could come with you into the land of fairy. I can lead you straight to the throne."

Autumn really wanted him to, but she shook her head. "I'll be able to sense the way. I want you back here, letting Lizzie know when there are fairies around. I've told her you'll come to find her at the church."

"The church?"

"The big pointy building with the bells."

"Oh. That thing." Trill, looking uneasy, nodded, and they set off.

The staff and teachers of the school locked up as quickly as they could and headed for home, taking the children with them that didn't have anywhere else to go. Lizzie asked Luke, Zoya, and Jas to come back to the Vicarage with her. "I'm trying to reach out with my extra senses," she said, "to see if I can feel even a slight flutter from any fairies. Trill gave me the same vibes Finn always did, but that was only when I was in the same room with them. At least I know what I'm trying to sense."

"What does it feel like, to have extra senses?"

"You get used to it," said Luke. "Handy around the house. Particularly for fixing plumbing."

"I can always feel something in the distance. And I feel like something good is watching over me."

"Me too." Which Lizzie realised had come out sort of wry.

"I didn't mean . . . I'm not religious."

"People do feel able to say two things like that back to back, don't they?"

"Let her off the hook," said Luke.

"Yes, let me off," agreed Zoya, who was studying Lizzie like she'd seen her for the first time. "Reverend. So, hey. Why didn't I get the whole deal with the rain?"

"I think," said Lizzie, "finding out why you weren't affected might turn out to be very important." Her phone buzzed with a text, and she looked at the screen. It took a moment of effort, knowing that a child was within earshot, to moderate what she said next. She scrabbled to hit the phone button.

———

Autumn was marching through the forest. She'd left Trill a few minutes before. He'd given her a last long-range forecast and all-clear. So it looked like they were right about this not being a mass invasion. They'd be massing on the border otherwise, right? She was, by her own reckoning, about half a mile from the point where the paths ahead were only perceptible to those with extra senses, where true fairy began. The invisible wall should be a lot closer, and indeed, now she was looking, ahead she could see a line of split and ragged trees.

Her phone rang. The display said it was Lizzie. Autumn had a momentary pang of awkwardness. They'd had such a nice parting, she hoped this wasn't going to be Lizzie telling her of all the extra reasons she'd thought of why she shouldn't go. She answered it. "Hi."

"You have to get out of there."

"Lizzie, there's nothing you can tell me—" There was a sound approaching, an enormous sound. What was that? Autumn put a hand over one ear and tried to concentrate on what Lizzie was yelling at her now. "What?" The sound was now getting closer, forcing her to look up. In front of her, she realised, the enormous trunks of the trees were bending, being forced to bow in her direction. As she watched, their branches began to explode like firecrackers.

"The wall!" bellowed Lizzie from the phone. "It's moving inward!"

Autumn realised that in a few seconds she'd be in danger from flying wood splinters. "Okay, got it!" she yelled, switched off the phone, and ran back the way she came. She stopped, panting, after a hundred paces or so, and looked back. Wait. The wall was moving slowly, seemingly being given pause as it pushed itself against trees and either heaved them over or made their trunks crumble with that weird explosive force it had.

So standing here she had a few minutes.

This . . . this was actually better. Now she didn't need to go sideways. Just down. She quickly pulled from her bag the camping spade she'd been given by the outdoor goods shop, extended its handle, and started to desperately dig.

———————

"What's at the centre of the town?" asked Lizzie, still staring at her phone and trying not to panic. In his text to her, the one that had made her call Autumn, Shaun had said he'd already told the Lychford WhatsApp and Facebook groups about the contracting wall, but she worried that still left literally hundreds of people at risk, in all directions. What happened when the wall started to hit houses?

"The church, of course," said Zoya. "Isn't that how it works in Britain too?"

"Oh," said Lizzie. "Yes, that's . . . probably true. Okay. Change of plans."

She found the first in her list of people to call and started sending out the word.

———————

Jake Tasker was one of the two burly sons of Erica, who was the landlady of the Folly pub, at the edge of town. He was a member of the rugby club, worked behind the bar, there and here, and was also a DJ for hire. He had a way with the crowds and he knew it, unafraid to play the whole of "Bohemian Rhapsody," yeah, from the start, when the mood was right. At this moment he was sitting at his mum's kitchen table, exhausted, quickly munching a bacon sandwich he'd thrown together while Mum took her turn with the crowds outside. They'd started using the chalk display boards to communicate with the masses, and now the authorities, the serious authorities, including someone yelling that he was from the Ministry of Defence, were out there. So they were a bit taken aback at what to do. When Jake had left it, Mum was trying to get through to the vicar and the witch to ask one of them to come down here. Jake still couldn't get his head around the idea that either of those two were the experts about all this. He felt that what the man from the ministry was probably going to reveal was that this was all some military operation gone wrong, some secret weapon that had misfired. All this stuff about invisible arrows . . . well, he didn't know anyone who'd got shot at. There was a USAF base a few towns away, you sometimes saw the bombers going over, and it was probably summat to do with them. That rain had probably been them all being gassed. Mind you, that might not be what anyone was revealing right now. That might take a big lawsuit. He'd argued about this with his elder brother, Nate, who believed in any old shit that drifted into his head, Jake often thought. He was absolutely on for this being magic and elves and ancient powers. Jake had told him to tell it to the dolphins when they showed up, 'cos it couldn't be long before they got in on this action.

Jake was just taking the first bite of his sandwich when he heard the weird sound from the wall behind him. It was as if it had started singing. It was sustaining a sort of high-pitched warbling. He looked over to the hearth. It was an old building, but he'd lived here all his life and he'd never heard anything like that. He put down his sandwich, went over to the fireplace, and put a hand to it. He could feel a tingling sensation, moving slowly up his arm. Not the whole arm, just a tiny bit, like his arm was moving through a scanner at the airport, though you couldn't feel those.

That was when his mum and his brother burst in. "Jake, get back!" shouted his mum, "It's the invisible wall, it's moving through the house!"

Jake realised that he could feel it on the front of his body now. It washed over his face. It must be a few feet in now, back from the fireplace. He wasn't afraid, because there was nothing to be afraid of. "It's all right," he called. He took an experimental step forward and felt the sensation wash completely over and past him. "I'm through," he said. "I'm on t'other side."

His mum and brother looked at each other, not sure they could trust this. "Well, stay there," said his mum.

"I'll walk behind it," said Jake. And began to do so as it crept forward. "It's not hurting the house, then?"

"No," said his brother, "it's gone straight over the stones we put down in the road, but it's messing up the grass on either side, so I dunno what the difference is."

"I'm hearing that from all over," said his mum, looking at her phone. "It's the same, the houses are fine."

"And I'm fine," said Jake. "Maybe we should all just walk through while we can?" He heard another sound from the chimney and turned to look. A cloud of debris had started to drift into the room. "We'd better keep a record of all the damage. So we can get the insurance onto this."

"You see if you can get through too," said Mum to Nate.

Nate nodded and stepped gingerly forward. He reached out a finger toward the barrier.

"Come on, you great tosser," said Jake. He grabbed Nate and hauled him through.

Nate screamed. That was all Jake was aware of in that second. A second later he was coughing, retching, stumbling, waving his arms blindly through a mass of burning debris that was all over him. He could hear his mother screaming too.

And as Jake slowly realised what had happened, he couldn't help but begin to cry out with her, to cry out in horror and despair, a sound he'd never heard himself make before.

The disintegrating mass of charred meat that was falling apart around him had, a moment ago, been his brother.

———————

Zoya didn't like the way that the reverend was looking. Lizzie had stopped in the street and was staring at the messages she was getting on her phone. "Some people are getting through the wall and some . . . aren't. Some . . . some really aren't. Oh my God."

Zoya looked over her shoulder and saw a photo she didn't want Jas to see. "It's sorting us. Into what? Is it an ethnic thing?"

"One of two brothers . . . one of them . . . he . . ."

"Keep it together, Reverend. We need you to—"

"Call me Lizzie. Why can't you call me Lizzie?"

"It's a sign of respect."

"But you don't feel that respect. You just think you should. And that's not the sort of respect I want, and you're obviously going to be someone important in all this and you were able to thump David Cummings. So. Call me Lizzie."

She'd only looked at her for the last part of that. Zoya realised that here was someone who'd also had to deal with quite some shit. And who had a shitload more on her shoulders right now. And who had a vibe about her that said there was something going on with her that she was still keeping inside. "Sorry," she said. "Call me Zoya."

"Like the Sorting Hat," said Jas.

"Yes, like that," said Zoya, looking to her. She looked back to Lizzie. "Only more dangerous."

"Well, the Sorting Hat was dangerous, sociologically—"

Luke loudly cleared his throat. "Is it time for that, do you reckon?"

Lizzie seemed to realise what she was saying and that her next words probably should be "in this essay I will" and visibly shut that shit down. "Sorry. Yes. It can't be genetic if it's one of two brothers. It must be something about the people. Something about their minds."

———

Autumn was digging deep. Literally and metaphorically at the same time. She was working the spade down through top soil, then through packed, dense earth, then into hardened tree roots. She kept going, though she could feel the sound of crashing trees getting nearer and nearer.

How would she know when she'd gone deep enough? Oh God, she wouldn't. The effect of the wall seemed physical. It couldn't be heaving soil and bedrock along down there, but it was definitely shoving small plants along in front of it, disintegrating them too. So it was being somehow selective. Maybe interrogating living things like plants as it went and easing its way through soil and stone. Like the arrows through the walls had been selective about the kinds of materials they could pass through. God, she was finding technological similarities in what the fairies would call "magic." Even if the laws of physics differed across the various lands next door to Lychford, she was still assuming that scientific principles, different versions of science, but still all based in rationality, applied throughout. That was what they'd found so far. Lizzie liked to say that Autumn had faith in the scientific method, but Autumn felt that if she encountered proof that this wasn't the case, some completely mixed-up world where no laws at all applied, or they varied moment to moment . . . anyway, Autumn knew she'd change her opinion when she encountered the evidence. To believe in and reach for the beyond was Lizzie's thing, and it suited her and was beautiful for her, an opinion of Autumn's which she didn't think Lizzie had ever quite believed she held. To ask the beyond some serious questions was Autumn's thing.

She was still digging while she was thinking, and she realised she'd got distracted. The sound and the feeling were looming above her now. The wall was right beside the hole. She still had a moment in which she could scramble out and run.

No. She had to go for it. Or she'd just have to dig another hole. She was pretty sure this one was deep enough. Pretty sure.

She flung herself flat, then spun, to be face up, because if she was going to get squashed, she didn't want it to happen arse-first. For some reason.

Then it was too late. She felt the great presence of the wall slide . . . oh God, it was touching her brow. She hadn't dug down far enough. She frantically tried to push herself back down into the soil as she felt something like a solid edge start to push into her scalp. Before she knew it it was past her eyeline. Sitting up now wouldn't be possible. And the back of her skull was flat against solid ground. But her nose was in the way of this thing. She couldn't turn sideways. The wall was shoved down too tight against her scalp. She couldn't help but reflexively try to scrabble and squeeze like a trapped animal to try to get out from under it, as it pushed hard at the bridge of her nose. There was a fizzing sense to it, an ozone hiss in her extra senses, as the wall seemed to make awful decisions about every particle of matter it encountered, and she was one of those particles, a small animal before this alien science that thought of itself as ancient and magical and important.

Oh God, the pressure was increasing. Was she going to lose her nose? She tried to get herself under control. Then she'd just have to take the pain. There wouldn't be too much blood, would there? Were there major arteries there? She hoped this thing would push down her breasts or she could squeeze under it or something.

She realised, as the pressure continued, that actually . . . was it . . . inside her nose now?

Yeah. The fizzing was inside her nose. She really wanted to sneeze. She held it in.

It was passing through her nose, harmlessly. And what was this feeling that went with it, something she'd actually felt from a few feet away from the thing, but hadn't interrogated at the time, the sensation that . . . it welcomed her? Approved of her, even? What the hell was that? A second later, it was out the other side of her nose. She panted with relief. She felt the wall slide past her chin and raised her head a little. She gritted her teeth and let it slide through her boobs, very much not appreciating the feeling of being judged at the molecular level, thank you, even if—no, *especially* if—the verdict were positive. Then she had the muscles of her shoulders free to work with and started slowly to pull herself back. And as it moved on, she could pull herself up, and finally out.

Autumn stood at the side of the hole she'd dug, gasping, on the other side of the wall. That thing had allowed her through. What was that about? She had no idea, and no time to interrogate the concepts. She looked back for only a moment more, then turned and started up the hill toward the land of fairy.

4

LIZZIE, IN HER URGENT series of phone calls, had told everyone to come to the marketplace, which was just down from the church, and so still pretty central. She'd told those she called to spread the word. Luke and Zoya had joined in by alerting all their contacts too. She was startled, however, when they turned the corner out of the lane, to see how many had got here. The area just south of the church was filling up with desperate-looking people, a lot of them with young families. And yet, given how big Lychford really was, with all the new builds and everything... oh God, had they really lost that many? There weren't many of those she'd met through her adventures with Autumn either. A couple from the Festival committee, a reasonable number from the W.I. Not so many from the pubs.

The crowd were by no means happy. There were loud voices and arguments, and when she'd appeared, she was sure she'd heard some ironic applause and even some boos. They'd gotten to that now? What, did they think this was her fault?

"A lot of noisy people," said Zoya, picking Jas up.

Lizzie saw Sue, her elderly church warden, making her way through the masses toward her. "Loads of people are getting through the wall," said Sue when she got to Lizzie. "My grandson Max saw one of his mates fall through it, and he was okay, and so he went through too. They're all texting their friends before they go through, saying who's gone before they did, because they know they won't be able to after. And once they're through, they can't get back in, it's just like a real wall from the other side. Except still invisible, you know what I mean. If you go up to the wall carefully, they're saying you get a sort of feeling about whether it's dangerous or not, but they've..." Lizzie realised the woman was trying not to cry. "A few of them have thought they'd be fine and..."

"So most people get through?" said Luke.

"Don't you start thinking like that," blurted out Sue. "Even if most do, there's a lot who don't, a lot!"

"It's okay," said Lizzie. "We're not going to try. It just explains why we're not packed in here."

"And," said Sue, "it's because the wall has stopped moving."

"What? Why would it do that?"

"You're the expert," said Sue. And Lizzie felt the slight criticism in her tone. "Are you going to hold some sort of service?"

"I . . . I don't think that's appropriate," said Lizzie, looking out at the crowd. Lots of her flock were indeed here, but this lot also included not just a large number of people she never saw in church, but also people of other faiths, like Sunil Mehra and that young woman with the market stall who'd once told Lizzie she was a chaos magician and seemed to want to start a fight every time she saw her. Lizzie hadn't actually encountered her since the realities of magic had been revealed to the whole community, and she'd had fantasies about trying not to be smug in her presence, but seeing her over there now, her mascara running from sobbing, felt specifically hard to bear. Which was surely a little note from God about that proposed smugness on her own part. She was really doing pretty badly right now in terms of honesty and not being angry and all the other things she was supposed to try harder with. Things were coming at her so fast . . . but no, she had to do better, that was all there was to it. If she dealt with her own failings, then other people's attitude toward her might get better too. Maybe. "I could do some sort of multifaith thing, but I think just all staying together and sharing what's happening would be more comfortable."

"Phew," said Zoya.

"Don't be mean, Mummy," said Jas.

"I like you," said Lizzie to the child, getting just a stoic nod in return. She turned back to Sue. "Okay, let's find some way we can address this crowd. And find out why this lot don't think they'd make it through the wall."

———————

Autumn had found the gateway to fairy, and it was in a sorry state. It stood past the point she'd come to regard as the edge of fairy territory, a little way in from the edge of the feeling of being off the beaten track and in someone else's property. She'd passed the ancient sign that indicated that roads other than those that appeared on maps were available. She could feel the well in the woods somewhere behind her.

The gateway was a series of strings of flowers that garlanded two trees, an oak and an ash. They hung between the branches to provide a rough entranceway. Autumn had worried about this place as a strategic point, that it'd be guarded, but she couldn't see any sign of that. The sense of the place was that it had been left to decay, the flowers now dry and lifeless, the strings thin. Maybe it was more of a custom to pass through here than a matter of geography. If she'd walked past rather than through, she felt she'd still get to fairy.

When she'd come through here as a young woman, she'd been blissed out of her mind. She'd been holding

Finn's hand. She'd been full of illusions. And other stuff. In all sorts of ways she'd believed in magic. The fear she'd started to feel on the other side, the sense of being lost, the terror at seeing Finn's father . . . that was where her doubt had started. She'd kept the good part of that doubt, made it her strength, even after she'd realised the experience had been utterly real.

She was a different person now. She could do this.

She didn't pause, didn't mark the moment, just started walking, and went straight through the gateway.

———————

Lizzie had decided to get onto the steps of the war memorial. She managed to get a reasonable amount of quiet, and she'd been trained in projecting her voice, but she could have done with a megaphone, or even her church's old P.A. system for what was looking like it could be a moment straight out of *Life of Brian*. "Okay," she called, "how many of you have approached the wall and felt you couldn't get through it?"

Loads of hands went up. Most of them.

"I think those who haven't had a go should try," said Lizzie. There was a buzz of consternation. "I don't mean you should take any risks. If you don't feel anything from the wall, then don't approach it." There was a lot of shouting in response. Lizzie managed to gather from people yelling over each other that several townsfolk had thought they got the feeling from the wall that they could pass through and paid for it. "Okay, so ... so ..." She looked over to where Zoya was holding Jas. The young woman had an expression on her face like she didn't know why Lizzie was even trying to talk to them. Luke was looking worried, like he thought this might all kick off in a second. She looked back to the crowd.

"All I'm saying is we should get as many people out as possible. Okay?" She was pleased to see a few of them heading off, acting on the advice she'd just given, advice she wasn't even sure of. The ones departing seemed generally more ... youthful, more the age group you'd see working in the supermarket or stand-ing in the shelter by the skate ramp in the park. Though, amongst them, she'd seen, to her surprise, Sunil moving at quite some speed. Those left here, those who'd come here, a lot of them were ... the old and the very young. That demographic was so familiar to Lizzie that it had taken her until now to realise that it was odd that they were the ones gathered here. These people fit the categories of those more likely to be churchgoers. And as she'd noticed, most of the actual churchgoers were indeed here.

So, reaching out with her extra senses now, concentrating on the difference in emotional texture between those leaving and those staying . . . and being aware all the while that they were waiting for her to say something instead of staring at them in weird silence . . .

Oh.

"Hands up," she said, loudly now, a lot more confident, "if you strongly believe in something. A religion, a political party . . . 'chaos magic,' anything beyond your friends and family."

Nearly all the hands went up. The members of the crowd looked at each other, now with a new worry to contend with but, thankfully, slightly more impressed with her.

"It's believers," said Zoya, having moved close enough to be heard from near the foot of the war memorial. "They've trapped all the believers. But didn't that rain make believers of you all?"

"Not so much. Autumn still thinks it's all about science we don't understand yet. Which . . . shit, if she tried, she'll have got through the wall." And this, she realised, was why they'd been allowed to keep their mobile phone signals. They'd needed to be able to talk to each other to gather like this.

"Reverend!"

Lizzie realised that was about her swearing. Which . . . okay, there was a child present. "Sorry. But shut up. Listen, now we know that, you should get out. Get away from here."

"Not without Jas," Zoya said calmly.

"Does she—?"

"Who's coming to visit at Christmas?" Zoya asked her daughter.

"Father Christmas," said the little girl.

"And who comes when you lose a tooth?"

"The Tooth Fairy."

Lizzie looked back to see all the other small children still in the crowd and nearly swore out loud.

———

The land of fairy had changed a lot. Autumn took one slow step after another, feeling as if every single thing might hurt her. There was a startling sense of unreality about the woods that, from what she recalled of her first time here, hadn't been a feature before. Sure, that experience had been dreamlike, but it had felt sensual, like the land had reached out and connected with her. It had been a bit like how her extra senses functioned now. But at the same time it had been its own thing. Now, though . . . this felt more like . . . a computer game. A violent, churning computer game where the landscape was rushing and reforming around her, threatening to break down completely at any moment. This felt dangerously close to being that cosmos she'd worried about where physical laws were unreliable. Behind her she could still see trees, but they were stretched, distorted. Ahead, the trees became like something in an impressionist painting. She got the feeling that soon they'd be just colours. The air seemed to be howling in her ears, without there being any wind, and the timbre of that howling changed depending on which way she turned. And the smell now, it wasn't more woodland than woodland, as she remembered from last time, it was more like . . . fire, industrial smoke . . . brimstone. That was surely not about hellfire, but more about . . . decay, maybe? Like rust? Was she smelling the decay of an entire reality? It was like Trill had said about belief underpinning these other realities, of something to do with minds being the machine code of other universes. Maybe not her own? Well, some of the discoveries of quantum physics, about how perception seemed to be important to reality—

She realised she was breathing too fast, that her mind had shied away into speculation because she was fundamentally not dealing with what was in front of her. Okay, okay, what could she rely on? She looked at her watch and watched seconds go past and timed her own heartbeat, which helped to calm her too. Right. Time seemed to be flowing at the same rate here as it did in her own world. Expectations to the contrary, that had always been the case for fairy. Individual fairies talked about time passing fast in the human world, but that was maybe more about their perceptions than about physics. Or if that was a change, it was one that would suit the enemy, because having time flow at the same speed everywhere was probably necessary if you were planning to mount an assault on several different planes of existence at once.

So, new rules had been imposed here, and they'd wiped over the ... code ... that had previously been in place. The rules might tend toward the orderly and practical, but they'd mushed up the experience of walking around here.

Therefore, it might actually be easier to find the castle. Where had the vast, weird, literally fairytale home of the king been? Previously, she wouldn't have even said that "where" was a suitable word. But now she could feel its presence as a gravity, right in the middle of this world. Of course. It would be, so now it was. The literal had encountered fairy and bolted it all down so they could make use of it.

And she could use *that*.

Autumn set off in pursuit of the obvious.

———

"So you're saying that because I ran for the council, because I believe we should be in control of our borders, I'm on the list to die?" A red-faced man in the crowd was shouting at Lizzie. Others were joining in, trying to explain their own passionate beliefs and why they shouldn't be held against them.

"I don't think it's trying to kill us." Lizzie was trying to make herself heard. "If it was, why did it stop, why didn't it just roll over us?" But now her voice wasn't carrying over the crowd. There were children here, and a lot of vulnerable elderly. She didn't want to turn this into a riot. "I'll get back to you when we know anything more," she said. "If your homes are still inside the wall, maybe you should go back to them. If not, I'm sure—" She'd been going to mention the coffee bars, but the hubbub had increased to the point where nobody was listening. Relieved, she let Zoya take her arm and hustle her away toward the church, Jas in one arm and Lizzie in the other. Zoya had quite some muscles, Lizzie realised. And the lack of giving a damn required to use her elbows to get past people. A moment later, Luke was beside Lizzie on the other arm, her literal wing man. He was a trifle more polite, actually apologising to the people they shoved past.

They went into the church and found Lizzie's office, where they could put the kettle on and close a door behind them, so at least any questions would be urgent ones. Lizzie went to find the kettle. "Well, I let them all down there."

"You did all you could," said Zoya. "These are the general public. The general public suck."

Lizzie appreciated the support, but couldn't quite bring herself to accept it. "So the enemy are concentrating the believers in one place. Which is maybe why the wall stopped moving. Perhaps it'd served its purpose."

Into the room, without knocking, strode Trill. He was looking worried.

"Where's Autumn?" said Lizzie.

"As far as I know, she continued on her quest."

"Then . . . yes. Okay. I won't be able to text her then. Okay."

"I was just thinking on my way back that you were having some weird weather here."

"Global warming," said Luke.

"Ah. Is that why there's something incredibly powerful building in the clouds up there?"

Lizzie was about to ask "oh God, is this it?" when she heard the sound of rain on the roof, the sound you only heard when that rain was coming hard and fast. And then, from outside, she started to hear the sound of screams.

———

Lizzie ran out of the church into the graveyard, the others close behind her. It was indeed raining hard, harder than she'd ever seen. It was like videos she'd seen on monsoons. But nobody gathered outside was running from it. Instead they were staring up into it. The expressions on their faces were ecstatic. They were holding their palms up to catch the rain, spooning it into their mouths.

Luke nudged her and pointed down. On the ground, the rain was already gathering in deep puddles on the uneven cobbles of the church path.

The rain was bright blue.

Autumn had started to see the castle in the distance. Sometimes it was suddenly in front of her, and sometimes it was far away, but she knew that was just her perceptions, while her feet, and her fear, told her she was getting steadily closer.

Her fear, yeah. Because this thing, this building, if it was truly a building, still had a hold over her, a terror deeper than the shifting mass of reality could create. She kept putting that aside, kept putting one foot in front of another.

There were still fairies here, but they were ... diffuse, intelligences that were always just over there, fluttering in circles, kept in cages within their own land. It was her difference, she was starting to realise, that let her walk here at all.

She kept the central horror of her life straight ahead and kept forcing herself to approach it.

———————

Lizzie had tried to pull some of those outside back into the church, but Zoya, Trill, and Luke had grabbed her and hauled her inside. She watched from the porch as more and more of those caught in the downpour were starting to look upward. Were they exulting in what the rain was doing to them, or were they seeing something up there?

"If . . ." Zoya said, standing beside her, "this last rain you had, which was not blue I take it, if that could get to you whether you were inside or not . . ."

This time Lizzie managed to restrain herself from swearing. "We don't know what it's meant to be doing. Can you feel anything weird?"

"No. Not yet."

"No," said Jas.

"Just that that's more fairy blood than I've ever seen, falling on the ground like it's weather," said Trill, sounding annoyed.

"I can feel something," said Luke. "I can feel . . . something great!"

And before they could grab him, he'd run out into the rain, and started to cry out, pointing joyously at the sky.

———————

Autumn was looking up at the castle. And now she was certain it wasn't really a building. It was something the fairies had built, yes, something that meant security and centrality to them. But it could equally have been a heart. As she thought that, horrifyingly, that was what it became—just for an instant. This thing was a metaphor that her mind, formed as it had been in a stew of postcolonial fear and anger, automatically translated as a seat of feudal power. But the power it contained was different to that which humans had tamed down into a soap opera about "royalty."

The fear, the knowledge of the illusion, however, made it easier to get inside. One needs to find a drawbridge or a window to enter a castle. How does one enter a heart? One begins anywhere.

And so Autumn stepped forward and kept taking steps, not letting her eyes lead her, but feeling the fear of what lay inside this heart or castle or concept and aiming herself straight for it.

"Oh God, I can feel it," said Zoya.

"I feel weird," agreed Jas.

"Tell me about it," said Lizzie to both of them. "Quickly." They were still all standing in the church porch, because Lizzie couldn't come up with any sort of plan to deal with this. The rain, she assumed, must have been created along with the dome, waiting up there as clouds ready to go when the container reached the right size, like some sort of ecological project.

"It's like . . . reading the tabloids at the Chinese take-away—the only time I read them," whispered Zoya, her pupils enormous. "It's all everyone else's fault. All *their* fault. Whoever they are. Something great is coming that will save me, and bring justice to all those who've wronged me, and make my little girl better, and everyone will get their just deserts. But . . ." And Lizzie saw her actually gritting her teeth. "My little girl can't 'get better.' She's fine as she is. I do not want to believe that. I do not believe any of it. Believing that shit is how I got here." And she actually slapped herself across the face.

"Don't, Mummy," shouted Jas. "Something great is coming! Father Christmas is coming!"

Lizzie hated the sound of enforced belief in the little girl's voice. She quickly performed a blessing over both of them, keeping eye contact with Zoya as she did so, and then added to it some basic protective spells that Autumn had forced her to learn. Oh God, she was performing spells now. She said the complicated words in what probably wasn't a real language several times, and then found, wonderfully, that Jas had joined in, seeming to find immediate comfort and support in the repetition. And then she started repeating Lizzie's blessing too. And then Trill joined in with some words of his own that sang with ancient power, and the little girl added them to the routine, looking up at her mother and grinning as she ran through the whole list over and over. "Father Christmas isn't coming," she said finally.

"No," said her mother, letting out a long breath. "No he is bloody not, not until Christmas Day. And this is not Christmas Day. And I very much want to thump something again for making me think like that."

Lizzie wanted to hug her. So she did. She didn't expect it to be reciprocated quite so warmly, so she quickly disengaged again. "I think we'll be okay if we go out there now. Do you want me to go first?" She was pleased to have done something useful and was desperately looking to sustain that, she realised. She was hoping that, in doing something helpful, she would find that she had some indication from her God about the contradictions she could feel increasingly underlined inside her.

Jas had gone to the doorway and was looking at the sky. Then she looked back to Lizzie. "You need to come out," she said.

———————

Autumn was doing her best not to scream.

She was at the very threshold of something that felt like . . . like an emotional black hole. Like her attending a fascist rally. It was someone else's passion that cared for her not at all, that saw her as an alien invader. As these increasingly powerful waves of emotion flowed over her with every step, what she was seeing varied from moment to moment too. If this was a castle, it was eating her. There were stairwells here it was impossible to climb back up. This was a woman-eating plant, a deadly flower, an amoeba, a trap.

This awful power was despised by its new owners, and yet it was still implicit and central in this world. Autumn wanted to burn it down. No, free it. Maybe free it while burning it down? She knew what was at the centre of it, and that had been bad enough last time, when all she'd had to face was this thing's own nature.

She thought, despairingly, about Lizzie asking her to come back. To run. That felt so important. But Lizzie, of all people, knew that wasn't the most important thing.

Protecting other people was the most important thing.

Autumn closed her eyes, closed her extra senses, too, started to climb, blindly, toward the gradient that would any moment drop her into oblivion.

Lizzie had carefully left the porch, Trill, Zoya and Jas with her, and, braving the rain, which now seemed to be lessening, looked up into the sky where now everyone, Luke included, was pointing. Lizzie hoped she could use the protective incantations on him, too, but it was going to take time they might not have.

Incredibly, Lizzie saw, there were figures in the sky. And they were descending. A group of three fairies. Behind them shone a golden light, and it was getting brighter and brighter. "I didn't know your lot could do that," she said to Trill.

"We can't," said Trill.

The descending fairies were armed, with bows, shields, swords. Perhaps these were some of the assassins who'd come after them. The expressions on their faces were calm, unworried.

Trill stepped forward, evidently furious to see his people like this. Zoya seemed to note that and squared her shoulders, ready to fight.

The fairies landed right in front of them. The people, the believers, all around, flocked quickly to them, but kept a little distance. Some of them had fallen to their knees in wonder.

One of the fairies that faced them suddenly jerked, and his face gained expression, so now Lizzie could honestly say he was looking at her. But she felt that whatever mind inhabited him it wasn't his own. "Hello again," the fairy said.

Lizzie realised with a shock that his voice was that of David Cummings.

"Yes, I'm awake again. Bit of a sore head. But it didn't put me out of action for long. The boss is on his way. So, you can save any more of your finnicky little words for the big man. Where's the other one?"

Lizzie realised he meant Autumn. "She got out, hopefully," she said. "Through your wall. She's gone to find help."

Which seemed to satisfy Cummings. Lizzie supposed that, if he had some way of knowing whether or not she was telling the truth, that test had been passed. "Then she's no concern of ours. But look, what's this? You have a fairy of your own. Ah. That must be how you escaped us. Well, he's been exposed to enough blood, let's get him back onside." He clicked his fingers.

Trill, to Lizzie's horror, seemed to react. But then he

recovered and raised an eyebrow. "I felt that. But it didn't work. You have no power over me, foul beast."

The fairy with Cummings' voice opened his mouth in shock. Then he closed it again. "Well. I'd now fry you like I did your prince. Except that might spoil the effect we're going for here. Moving on. Time to meet the boss."

An enormous sound came from the sky.

Lizzie had always distantly had, in the back of her mind, some idea of the end of the world. She suspected the younger generation felt it even more than she did. There was, of course, a thread to her religion about the Kingdom, and what would happen at the end of everything. But keeping one's eyes on that was a trap she'd seen a lot of her folk fall into. She'd always preferred the sort of Christianity that worried more about what was going to happen at the food bank on Monday.

And yet, despite all her protections, despite the specific power of her own faith, or perhaps because of it, she felt the enormous thing that was now coming down in exactly the way the enemy expected her to feel it.

She could see it too. It was descending through the sky like its heralds had, presumably through the wall above, billowing in clouds of what could well be fairy blood.

It was an angel. An enormous, destroying, completing angel.

It had four faces, one on each side of its head. The light

haloed around that head, framing it exactly like something out of a medieval painting. The faces were golden, the eyes empty, the expression on each mouth a placid smile. The angel wore armour, and a fluttering tabard, on the front of which was emblazoned a lion. The angel carried a flaming sword.

Lizzie felt herself reacting not so much to the imagery, but with her extra senses. Which this being must be broadcasting to, as well as through the blood. She looked quickly to Zoya. "What can you see?"

"Big Marvel superhero propaganda."

"Father Christmas," said Jas. "Fake Father Christmas."

So they could see it, too, despite Zoya not even having the benefits of the first rain, the one from the well in the woods. This thing was really ticking all the boxes. Lizzie looked to the crowd across the churchyard and marketplace. Among those ecstatic faces were surely many who didn't believe in a Christian end of the world, in any end of the world, but whatever this was was enthralling them too. Cummings had said something about individually tailored fantasies, hadn't he? So presumably they were all seeing what they wanted to see. Not every religion believed in an end of the world, but then, you didn't get many Buddhists in Lychford. She wished she could ask Sunil, but he hadn't returned. Perhaps he'd got through the wall. She looked back up, guiltily aware that she'd been trying to distract herself from her own increasing feelings of religious awe.

Above her was coming loyalty and reward and justice. It was, despite everything, welcome. It was making her want to cry just looking at it, to cry not in fear, but in horrid exuberance, like a baby crying on the breast of its mother. The feeling made her feel excited and sick at the same time. She could hear actual cheering from some of the crowd, on top of a lot of sobbing. "I . . . didn't," she managed to say, looking back to the fairy that was channelling Cummings, "expect your boss to look like that."

"Yeah," said the fairy, "he gets that a lot."

The gigantic being dropped deftly onto his sandaled toes in the graveyard, right next to the statue of Pipkin the church cat that had, for a brief and glorious six weeks, been the central feature of Pokemon interest in the little market town. As Lizzie watched, the being shrunk, with a noise like a reverse orchestra, down to being just a little bit taller than anyone else.

The four faces contemplated the crowd. Here was the ultimate headmaster, hard but fair. Here was someone to be feared. Here was someone to be adored. Lizzie felt enormous emotion wash over her, over all the crowd. This was like . . . patriotism, an enormous good feeling at being part of something that was in itself unquestionably good. This was the feeling that everyone assumed Lizzie felt all the time, but it was actually the feeling her entire training had been about distrusting the taste of.

This being was bigger to her extra senses than any she had ever encountered. Silence fell. They were all waiting for it to speak.

And then it inclined its head to look at her.

"Lizzie," the voice said. And it was as warm and golden as the light of the flaming sword as it fluttered over them all. Lizzie was startled, flattered, horribly, that it was addressing her directly. "You've worked so hard. But the end is here. Justice is here. Even Lucifer has played his part, as is ordained." He nodded toward the fairy that was channelling Cummings. "I am here to divide the good from the evil. I am the alpha and the omega, the end of all conflict, the end of the world."

Lizzie wanted desperately to fall to her knees, as a lot of people around her already had. She looked to her friends. Zoya had one eyebrow raised, her hands over Jas's ears, unimpressed. Trill was furious. Luke was sobbing in wonder.

She looked back to the angel. Every cell in her body was saying that it was her job now to submit to divine judgment, to give herself up to the ecstasy she could feel waiting for herself and everyone around her. Here was blissful completion. All she had to do was give in.

She looked back to Cummings. There was a suppressed glee on the face of the fairy he inhabited, a smugness. They were trying to sell her and everyone else on an idea of what this was. They were hoping her emotions, her zeal, would get the better of her rationality.

Lizzie took a moment to compose herself. She stepped forward and addressed herself to one of the angel's several faces. "Bollocks," she said.

———————

Autumn was making her way down some stairs. Or was inside the cavities of someone's body. Or was in a cave. Her absolute assurance that each was true changed every moment. Ahead of her she could hear a sort of white noise which might be a voice. It was perhaps getting incrementally clearer. The terror, on the other hand, was all around her.

Autumn didn't want to reveal her presence, but at the same time, she had a feeling this was the voice of the being she had come to see. There was a tune in her head she'd never forgotten, one Finn had always sung or whistled when he'd strode jauntily across the border from the summerland. She tried it now, whistling it, a high, repetitive, six-note strain followed by a recurring three-note summons. Well, that was the closest she could get with her human voice. She hoped it was perhaps some sort of signal, or at least an indication that she was familiar with some of the local customs.

The moment she started whistling, the sound ahead stopped.

Before Autumn could react further, the nature of what she was walking through changed. It changed from diagonal to vertical.

Suddenly this black hole was a pit, and Autumn was falling.

The angel was staring at Lizzie, as if it still couldn't quite believe what she'd said. A lot of the townsfolk couldn't either; they were already calling for her to shut up. "Lizzie!" hissed Luke, astonished. There were some furious rants being directed at her from all sides, but Lizzie ignored them and kept her eyes fixed on this being that was doing its best to make her shiver and exult.

"You're not welcome here," she said.

"Oh, but I am," said the warm voice. The angel indicated the people all around, who were indeed nodding and looking angry at her.

"To give everyone their just deserts. Revenge and reward. Who here deserves better than they have had?"

There were a lot of shouts in the affirmative. "It's lying," she called. "All it can offer you is death. Don't you remember? It already killed a lot of your friends and relatives with that wall."

"My wall selected those who are to be saved," the angel replied, still ferociously calm. "Each to their own reward. There is no death now. They have all just gone on ahead." Someone somewhere was singing "Jerusalem." Ecstatic cries were starting to come from everywhere.

"I have been told," she called, "directly told, by these beings, what is really going on here. They're trying to take over our world."

"Lizzie," sighed the angel. "Lizzie, I know it's hard. You've been so alone. Because you couldn't face the alternative. I have tested you. And you have not been found wanting. What you were told, that was a story. You've been led up the garden path by your friends, the witches, quite a few times, haven't you? Just because you heard what sounded like the truth, a truth you held onto, doesn't mean that's how things are going to be. There aren't going to be any big revelations that matter now. *This* is the revelation. It's time for all these good people, who've all suffered so much, to get the fruits of their hard work. It's time for them to get back everything they've lost."

"You're full of shit," called Zoya. But there were now lots of much louder voices calling for her to shut up. Luke got up to look threateningly at her, but Trill stepped forward and he backed off.

"If enough of you want it," the being continued, "if you all say out loud to me that you want it, I can bring down all the barriers between worlds, and you will all be together, as one, forever. All your beloved dead will be returned to you. There will be no more secrets. Just one land, united, forever."

People around her were calling out their approval. Lizzie desperately looked around for dissenting faces in the crowd. She found a few, but only a few.

"That's why they filtered out the nonbelievers," said Zoya. "They were concentrating you all here, ready to do this. Maybe nonbelievers are harder to con."

"Or," corrected Lizzie, "maybe they have less power to offer. But yes. This is also why the assassins only zapped one of Autumn and me, but made sure we both felt threatened enough to bring everyone together. They probably thought I'd be under their control so they could use me to help finesse that."

"If you want paradise, a solution to all things," the angel was saying to the crowd, "you must gather everyone worthy and then all say it together out loud."

"Clap if you believe in fairies," whispered Zoya.

"I will return, in an hour, to find you all assembled here and ready for your reward," continued the angel, to cries of disappointment. "Then you will all give your assent with one voice, and everything will be perfect."

The glow around it intensified, and, to more cries of woe, it vanished.

The fairy with Cummings's presence inside glanced at Lizzie. "Don't try anything," he said. "We'll be watching." And then his expression left and the face was blank again. The possessed fairies all moved as one and went and stood together in line, ready to act should they be required.

Lizzie felt the absence of her God like a stone in her heart. She felt as if whatever message he'd had for her had already come and gone. And here was the enemy disregarding them now, as if they could do nothing further to hamper its plans. What could they do in an hour?

"They're going to vote yes," said Zoya. "Talk about exactly the right offer. They're giving the bloody English a chance to live in the past. Oh God, who's this now?" She was indicating the road up from the marketplace.

Lizzie looked in that direction. Sunil Mehra was running toward the church.

Trill stepped forward as if this could be an attack. But before Lizzie could tell him that this was a friend, probably, the fairy spasmed. He nearly fell to the ground. But then he staggered to his feet again.

Sunil slowed down, looking surprised at what he could see ahead of him.

Trill pointed at the restaurant owner and screamed.

———————

Autumn hit the ground. She'd been screaming, expecting to die. The end of the fall had been a complete surprise. The floor caught her and prevented her from harm. And yet it was like being caught by a warm predator. She was still in darkness, but now she was in the bosom of something, that sound of life now a whisper that was right in here with her, and she was held fast in . . . no, as quickly as she'd had that thought, she was lying there with nothing holding her.

There was enormous presence in this perfectly dark . . . chamber. Yes, it felt like a room. The whispering remained on the edge of earshot but the reverberation of it suggested an enclosed space with amazing acoustics. Gradually, the whispering faded. The presence became the silence. It was like the moment in a classical music track before the orchestra started playing. When you could just feel them there. She became very scared of how the voice that must come would sound. "Hello?" she began, breaking the silence herself.

A small voice, right in her ear, asked her who was there.

"Ahh!" she yelled, leaping up.

The voice asked again.

"Autumn Blunstone," she said quickly. "Wise woman of Lychford." That was the first time she had assigned herself that title. Though she guessed it was implicit. But it had always felt before that that name still belonged to Judith. She felt suddenly bad that she'd done that now, out of a desire to somehow defend herself against being in the power of the thing all around her.

The voice hardly reacted. It told her it was asleep. That all meaning was gone. That it was going again. And then it was gone and the whispering began again.

"I'm here to wake you up," said Autumn. But there was no reply. She was pretty sure she was in the presence of the king, because just over there ... yeah, she could feel the enormity of him. There was no physical component to that size. He was a conceptual hugeness. Like a galaxy. Like a theory.

And what was this in here with him? There was some sort of ... extra idea in here, something inserted, that hadn't grown in this space. Only it was now forcibly associated with the enormous presence. Oh ... this must be whatever the enemy were using to influence the king, to poison his blood, to make him broadcast the controlling fantasies to his people.

Autumn moved around the space, trying to feel the limits of it, but she could find none. She couldn't put her hands on some sort of device to smash it. Whatever magic had put it there was beyond her. So, she couldn't start to clean the king's blood. Back to plan A. She reached into her bag, feeling increasingly desperate. How had she ever hoped to wake an idea with a potion? Nevertheless, she found the bottle. She couldn't even see the container, never mind any sort of mouth to pour it into. In her heart of hearts, she didn't want to wake him up, because that would mean giving him existence, and she remembered what that existence was like, from the glimpse she'd had all those years ago. And here she was inside his heart. Inside that hugeness. Waking him would bring the old terror. Waking him might be the end of her.

But no, that didn't matter.

Distracted, she found her sweating hands slipping on the bottle. She grabbed for it.

The bottle fell. Horrified, Autumn heard it shatter.

———

Zoya had stepped forward immediately, aiming to get between this new arrival and Trill, whose bellow she'd initially taken for rage. But now the fairy's expression had changed to one of fear, and pain. Uniquely among the fairies, who were otherwise still blandly staring straight ahead, Trill had been somehow enormously affected by the man's arrival. The fairy was stumbling, still trying to point, but looking on the point of collapse. All control, in every sense of the word, seemed to have left him. "I have . . . a message," he said, in a voice which sounded like making the shape of the words had been an effort.

"What is it?" said Lizzie, going to him and putting a hand to his face.

Zoya looked to the crowd. Of course, they were listening intently to every word. They were very interested in any message that might impact upon their deliberations about immediately saying yes to the first glowing person who'd asked them if they'd like the world to end. The new arrival, who Zoya was pretty sure she recognised from the Indian restaurant, was looking at them all in utter bafflement.

She looked back as Trill slapped Lizzie's hand away, an entirely different expression settling on his features. Then he pushed past them all like someone climbing out of a hole and went to look more closely at the new arrival.

"I just went to lock up my restaurant," said the newcomer. "I have no idea what's going on."

"Us neither," said Lizzie.

Trill gave a sudden shiver. Then his whole posture changed. He stopped shaking, and adopted a slight stoop. He looked around with a wry sort of puzzlement and slight displeasure on his face. Then he found the restaurant guy again and he smiled. "Sunil," he said. "There you are."

"Why is he impersonating an old lady?" asked Zoya, now at the peak of her tolerance for weirdness.

"Oh my God," said Lizzie. "That's Judith."

5

AUTUMN WAS DESPERATELY, ridiculously, on her hands and knees, looking for the remains of the bottle, for the wetness of the liquid that had been inside. She couldn't find it. It was gone beyond gone.

She slowly straightened up.

She'd had her little plan. But plans would not suffice here. Not here at the end of everything.

Here was the time for the greatest sacrifice. It was all she had. The king needed new blood. She had that.

She carefully felt inside her bag once again, and her fingers closed on the hilt of her penknife.

Lizzie watched in amazement as Sunil Mehra slowly backed away from a fairy who, with the shuffling motion of an old lady, seemed to be advancing on him with romantic intentions.

The crowd of locals were dealing with this with a mixture of awkward puzzlement and annoyance that this was kind of getting in the way of the end of the world. "This is a frigging joke," the red-faced man from before was saying. "We just have to say yes. All of us. We just have to say yes together. Say it with me now." A lot of the crowd joined in with him. "Because what happens if we don't? The end of the world without us? The rewards for someone else?" Lizzie was relieved that the crowd seemed to have decided to ignore this little sideshow. And the fairies hadn't woken up either.

"I think," Lizzie whispered to Zoya, "that Judith might have left the heart behind as some sort of hidden preparation against this invasion. I think we might be about to hear some sort of important message that could save us."

"Great," said Zoya. "Who's Judith?"

"This is an important message," said Trill, in Judith's voice. "For my boyfriend."

"Oh fuck," said Lizzie. But still. Still. Whatever this was would be worth hearing. "Let her touch you," she called to Sunil.

"Really?" said Sunil. But he stayed put.

"That's Judith!" Luke called out, excitedly. "Judith Mawson! Communicating with us from the afterlife!"

"So we get to hear what's what from the horse's mouth," said one of the ladies from the church down the road that was kept at a bit more ecstatic a temperature than Lizzie liked to keep St. Martin's.

"She'll tell us what's waiting for us up there," added Luke. Lizzie held back an urge to slap him.

Judith/Trill had now reached Sunil and was stroking his hair. "This is a recorded message," she said.

"It's not that I mind . . . you know," Sunil said. "It's just that this isn't . . . isn't Judith and I don't know how or who—"

"It's a fairy," said Lizzie.

"I would never use that word," said Sunil, desperately.

"It's me," said Trill, in Judith's voice. "And if you're hearing this, I've kicked the bucket. You see," and Lizzie realised that she was indeed sounding chatty and completely out of context for the situation, as a recorded message would be, "one day on the edge of town, I found a poor fairy dying. He were lying under a tree branch. There'd been a storm the night before and the branch must have landed on him. Anyway, I didn't know how to make him right, and he weren't in no state to tell me, so I did what I could to preserve his life. I used a lot of spells, and concentrated his whatnots all in one place, put some enormous protections on him so nothing could hurt him by way of infection and those who wished ill to him couldn't find him, and reduced him down to summat he could grow eventually back from."

Lizzie realised he . . . or she . . . was talking about the heart. And now they knew why Trill hadn't been affected by the poisoned blood.

"I thought," continued Judith, "that one day I'd learn how to grow him back. But as I got older, I started to think 'this fairy fellow is going to outlive me,' so I made a note to myself to tell whoever was due to take over from me all about it. I'm hoping either me or her's told you all about the secret stuff of Lychford, Sunil, or you'll be thinking I've lost it."

Sunil seemed to be believing what was in front of him now. He reached out and grabbed Trill's hands, holding onto them and looking into Trill's eyes as if he could see more of Judith there.

"I'm sure I'll have made sure all that's happened before this gets delivered. I'll have seen to it. I'm going to give that fairy heart to whoever this apprentice I've chosen is, right at the end of my life when I know I'm on my way out, and explain what it's all about, and say it includes a message for you, Sunil, and if that's the way this has gone, I'm glad, because you'll be ready to hear what I have to say to you. If that hasn't happened, for some reason, the heart will come straight to you, soon after I pop my clogs, because I've made a magical arrangement with the post office. Not that they know anything about that. There'll be a powerful suggestion with the heart for you to seek out a source of magical power. I can only hope that person knows how to bring a fairy back to life."

"Judith forgot to tell us about it," whispered Lizzie, amazed and sad. "Because of her dementia. Or maybe she just thought it was none of our business."

"You've got a lot to fill me in about," said Zoya.

"So the message is this, Sunil," said Judith. "I always loved you."

"Oh," said Sunil. "Oh no. Please, no, Judith—" He sounded like he thought this wasn't quite proper. For most of the time he'd known her, of course, Judith had been a married woman. One he'd flirted outrageously with, but still. "I'm sorry I was never your boyfriend. Not really."

"You were my sunshine. You were my escape from the obligations I'd fallen into. You never judged, even if what I was saying sounded loopy. So I'm quite pleased to think of your face now. I can see it in my mind's eye. And in a minute, after this message is recorded, I'm going to go over and see you for real and order a chicken korma extra mild and some chips and you're going to ask me what I've been doing today and I'm going to say I was preparing a fairy heart. I hope you'll remember me being so daft. I hope I finally got to say summat like I just did to you while I was still alive. But if not . . . well, now you know."

"I remember," said Sunil to Lizzie. "I remember her doing that." He quickly looked back to Trill. "I remember you doing that, Judith. I—" Lizzie realised he'd started to cry. "Why couldn't you tell me all this while you were alive?"

"Now," continued the voice of Judith, oblivious to his words, as Trill turned on the spot, the fairy's eyes looking around the crowd on autopilot, "the other person who might get to listen to this is anyone who's been chosen to guard Lychford. Maybe it's my apprentice. If so, hello, love. I hope you haven't been stupid enough to summon me as an intercessional presence. You need to be your own wise woman, not rely on imaginary copies of me."

Lizzie wondered if, in the absence of Autumn, she should step forward. But Judith's gaze swept straight past her.

"Or maybe I'm not talking to my apprentice. Maybe it'll be my apprentice's apprentice, the next in line, if this takes a while to get heard. At any rate, it'll be someone the land all about has chosen. The shape of the town often has a say in who the wise woman is, or so I was told when I was initiated." To Lizzie's surprise, Trill suddenly seemed to fix on a direction and marched over to address Zoya. "Right. This message is for you."

Zoya stared at the fairy, looking startled. "What? No. I know less than any of them."

"I hope we've had a proper handover," Judith continued, "and that all my magical whatnots have been passed down to you. You should feel known by the shape of the land now. Loved by those you can't see and never will."

Lizzie realised that she'd heard Zoya say something like that. But Zoya was stridently shaking her head. "No."

"You'll take your power from the map of the town, and your home will be your place of greatest strength, as it was for me. Until I spoiled it for myself. And had to live with a ghost because of my foolishness. Don't you be a fool. If you can manage that."

"I like her, Mummy," said Jas.

Lizzie saw the look of bafflement on Zoya's face suddenly become one of shock. "Oh," she said. "Oh." Then she looked to Jas. "Are you okay to stay with the rev … with Lizzie? Mummy back in five minutes."

Jas nodded.

"Where are you going?" asked Lizzie.

"I have a ridiculous thought," said Zoya. "And I don't want to hear the rest of that message until I have looked into ridiculousness." And with that she turned and jogged off the down the street, pulling her phone from the pocket of her jeans.

Lizzie looked back and saw Trill slump into inactivity, waiting for the recipient of his message to return. The crowd sighed. Lizzie checked her phone. They had forty minutes left before the end of the world.

———————

Autumn had had a ridiculous idea, a terrifying idea, and here she was in the dark implementing it. She'd remembered what Trill had said about the compatibility of human and fairy blood. If she was right, she had a way to make a sacrifice not to one of the great powers, who might not want to venture into the place she was, might not even be on her side in the current conflict, but to the king himself. She put the knife to her lips, happy now that she kept it sterilised with boiling water. Not being able to contain a wince, she drew it down across her flesh. The cut was too sharp to feel. A moment later her mouth was full of the taste of her own blood. A lot of it. Oh God. Drips were already pouring to the floor.

She put the knife back in her pocket, feeling like a proper witch but, however, acutely aware of how badly she'd wounded herself.

She used her tongue to make sure her blood covered her lips. Wow. None more goth than she. She was proud to be that in the belly of the beast.

She stepped forward, reached out, was open, seeking. She tried to find the king.

———

Zoya was hoping against hope that the house she needed to get to was still inside the wall. She had to look on her phone to find it, and it must be perilously close to the edge. She headed north, to this place she had often heard talk of but had never been to. She realised as she approached, though she had less of a feel for this than the people who talked about having extra senses, that she'd been lucky.

19 John Wittingham Road, without the first "h," was still inside the wall.

She slowed as she walked along the estate houses with gardens that varied between neat and untended. Here was an ancient car being taken apart. Here was a modern one that had rusted. Ahead she could feel a place that was standing out now she was this close.

This was the love that she'd always felt from the north of the town. The care from something invisible that Judith had spoken about.

She had never come to seek it out, because before that would have seemed ridiculous. She had never come to this address because she had never had time. She had never realised that the two things were one and the same.

Here was the house. It was a perfectly ordinary house. The garden didn't attempt to achieve much. There was no sign of children's toys, and no car. It looked like a pensioner lived here. And yet whatever was inside the building was singing to her now she was this close, wanting to give itself to her, like she was sixteen again and this was her first disco and the world was suddenly afire with expectation.

Could it be? Could the error in the magic be this small, this stupid, this human? She had seen, in that dream world, while that shitty man had been unconscious, that vision of Lychford that was projected on the wall there. In that the addresses were all jumbled, all needed translation. Perhaps that was how the supernatural authority that automatically bestowed whatever Judith had thought was going to be bestowed on the basis of geography could get equally confused by a human map. Perhaps the mistake of a county council could have consequences on stages way beyond those the councillors could imagine.

She saw that the front door was open. It didn't feel like an invitation. The door was moving slightly in the chill wind.

She went quickly up the path, ignoring the fear because there were others to fear for. She pushed open the door and went inside.

Autumn's senses found the king. She told him that she had blood, clean blood, fresh blood, all her blood, to freely offer him. And then there was something terrifying in her arms. She was holding the power of a sleeping cosmos. It decided on a mouth and made it. It was an entire people. It was here at one point just for a moment, for her now. It was warm and desperate and needed her like nothing ever had.

Autumn kissed the king of the fairies and fed him with her blood.

———————

Zoya had called out in the hallway, to no response. The cold had got into the house. Now she was inside, the feeling of being here in the heart of something she'd never known she'd lost was even stronger. It was like . . . coming into an inheritance. No, that was wrong. It was like inheriting something wonderful made from love. Except this hadn't been given deliberately. But neither had it been withheld. Not deliberately. Not quite. This wonder simply hadn't known about her, hadn't seen her.

Yeah, right. Maybe it should have bloody searched harder.

Was she supposed to . . . move into this house? No. It was clear someone already lived here. Oh. There were extraordinary, livid paintings on the walls. They all looked like they'd been painted by the same person, and there were too many of them. They were struggling to all fit.

They made a mess of the space. What they depicted . . . some were pictures of Lychford, and there were some other landscapes, yearning ones, pictures of the places you go to in dreams.

All the paintings felt . . . like they were missing something. There was some corner of each of them that needed extra weight, some imbalance that made you tilt your head. That was perhaps why there were so many of them, an attempt to make quantity fill the gap that would never be filled. Zoya put her hand to the surface of one of them, as if it could connect to her, as if she could add to it. That didn't seem that big an as if. But nothing happened.

She went into the next room, the living room, and there he was.

The old white man was lying on the carpet, on his face, both arms straight out in a ridiculous, undignified, fall. He was dead. The cold filled the room and had entered him too.

In his back were two arrows.

Oh. Oh damn them. The assassins had come here in error. When they should have come for her. They had made that same stupid mistake as the cosmic authority of Lychford had. Then they had realised and had gone to wait for her at the school. They had hoped to control this man. But that body looked so thin, his limbs so frail, he hadn't survived the attempt.

She went to him and lay down beside him to see his face. He looked half-caring and half-angry. He looked halfway between everything. His expression said he was still missing something. That he remained incomplete. Even though he was over. She should hate him for having kept a power and knowledge that could have been hers. And she did, a little. But he hadn't done anything with what he had. He hadn't understood it. All his art said that. He had always been missing something. He had never become wise.

But now she could.

Zoya couldn't help it. She reached out and touched the man's face.

And something was completed.

———————

Autumn found the kissing was something she'd needed. She'd gone all the way into the heart of what she feared the most and had found what was there and held it against her bosom and given all she was to it. She felt the kiss taking all the blood from her, taking all she had, but she'd had to suckle this enormous galaxy beast, she'd had to force it to take it, it hadn't forced anything on her. She had never felt so strong. It had taken her willingness to sacrifice everything, but she had no doubt anymore. She was the wise woman of Lychford.

She understood, distantly, that the king's eyes were open. It was like light spilling into a darkened room. But then they closed again. He was lost in despair. He could not find a spark of emotion to bring him back. Their poison kept on pumping into him, and she didn't have enough blood to counter it completely.

She found her body again, found her hand, shaking with the lack of blood. She found sensation in her hand and made it, full of pins and needles, reach into her bag.

Her hand closed on the terrible thing she'd brought with her.

———————

Zoya stood up, feeling authority and acceptance racing through her. She felt the completion, the love of the land. She felt she could put her hand now on that thing she'd always known in the distance, but had only started to grasp when she'd come here. The hedge witch, the words said, would come to live in Lychford, and would balance the space between what was and what could be. These words were not her own. But a moment later they were.

The rain that had come from the well in the woods, whatever that was, had thought it had nothing to teach her, had thought she had already inherited her potential.

The rain had *thought*! It hadn't known that the shape of the town and the land had been broken, that she had arrived at the right time but had found the potential split and mistaken. Her mother had prepared her. Her mother had half known. All those books had contributed. There was still a long road in front of her. She was the new apprentice and she had to find the wise woman and tell her she was ready now.

"Oh," she said to herself, and now to a whole new world that was listening, "I am so going to kick that angel's arse."

———

Autumn waited for an unknowable time.

In the space where she was with the king, she had put the head of the king's son.

She gradually started to feel it. His anguish finally roared from him like the tide on the beach. What had done this? How had he allowed this? What had become of him *to* allow this? He was wanting to have the energy to do something, he was willing himself to, he was not going to be able to defeat the terrible otherness that had infected him. The tide was being dragged back from the beach.

Autumn let the blood flow from her lips and willed him to take it all.

———————

Lizzie had decided that the best thing she could do right now was to try to get through to Luke. Because even Sunil, who'd gone to wait beside Trill as if he might hear more from Judith, now had a distant look about him, as if he was being swayed by the blood that filled the air. So she really wanted to see if she could get through to someone. She made sure Jas was okay, told her to stay by the church porch, then went to Luke, grabbed him by the shoulders, and led him forcefully away from the others. "Look at me," she said. "What is it you want?"

"What are you doing? Stop getting in the way. I just want everyone to be together and happy."

"How is that going to happen?"

"If you stop arguing and let it happen."

"But I'm not going to be happy if this happens."

"Then that's your fault."

"But I thought you wanted everyone to be together and happy?"

He just angrily shoved her aside and went back to join the others in their excited anticipation of what the angel was going to do when it returned.

Lizzie wanted to fall to her knees. So she did. She looked at the pools of blood all around and decided she didn't want to see that. She closed her eyes and prayed for her friends, for everyone in the this town and in the universe that now had twenty-five minutes left.

———————

Autumn was finding her fear getting smaller and smaller, as her awareness got smaller. She'd given a lot of blood now. The king, in such a small space with her now, was awake, was sobbing, was just like her, full of loss and sorrow.

What had they done to his boy?

He would make it up to him. He would make it well again. He would make things well for everyone.

But he was not quite yet awake. These were only the desperate wishes of an old man.

Autumn was pleased that she had found out what she was. Like her and unlike. But he was what she knew. So well. And so, she realised, she had something she needed to do to complete this working, this largest working, this working that could save everything. "I won't die for you," she said, wiping the blood from her mouth. "I can't do this for you. If you want to save him, if you want to save everyone, you need to do it yourself. You need to wake up."

He was angry at her now. Increasingly angry. The fury hit her full on.

Autumn fell to the ground and smiled with bloody teeth. To be angry, you need to be awake.

———————

Lizzie realised that she could hear something different. She opened her eyes. Had the angel returned early? No. It was the fairies who'd been on guard. They were reeling, stumbling, crying out. All except Trill, who was still standing there passively being Judith.

She leapt up, went to the nearest fairy, and grabbed his hands. After a moment, his eyes started to focus on her. It was as if he was trying his hardest to wake up. "Oh Autumn," she whispered, "you did it."

From across the way came a shout. Lizzie saw that Zoya was running toward them. She was gesturing at the sky. "They're going for it early," she yelled.

Lizzie looked up, and indeed, the light had returned, and, to the wild applause of the human beings below, the angel was forming out of the clouds once more.

"Oh no," said Jas, coming over to calmly stand beside her. "Father Christmas."

Of course. Whether or not Autumn had woken up the fairy king and freed the fairies from sleep, Cummings still controlled the humans through the same blood. Maybe the fairies weren't onside anymore, but Lizzie was pretty sure the angel didn't actually need them.

———————

There was now a place in the space inside fairy where the king, awake, had put Finn's head. Enormous energies of growth were all around. New rules of physics were being formed every moment. Autumn lay there, numb, watching, delighted, on the edge of death herself. As she observed, Finn was being grown again, was having his consciousness put back into a new place of being that, as with last time, was beyond the physical ideas of humans.

She had no idea how she was going to get out of here now. She was horribly worried about breaking her promise to Lizzie. She wouldn't give all her blood to the king. He had indeed got there on his own. She had not completed the sacrifice, because it was not her job to sacrifice herself for him. But she still didn't have enough left to keep going. She decided that she wanted to keep on speaking. She hadn't finished. "It can't be like it was," she said. "They tore up all those rules. We need new ones. Ones they can't tear up. Ones that won't leave us all vulnerable to our own mistakes."

The king told her he was listening, while he was making. He owed her. Enormously. He would repay.

Autumn barely heard him. She realised she could

ask to be healed with these enormous energies he again had access to. But no. One wish. No. She had to keep talking. This was more important. "My land is just the place I am. Yours is the place you are. I want a new deal between all the worlds. For the bad guys too. No more borders."

The king was silent. And as she strained to hear a reply, Autumn found herself slipping away.

———————

Trill suddenly jerked and pointed again at Zoya, once again adopting Judith's stoop and voice. "And if I'm talking to my apprentice or the apprentice of my apprentice this is just to let them know: you basically just have to bloody make it up as you go along. All right. I love you, Sunil, you silly old man."

Sunil didn't reply. He just closed his eyes and kissed Trill on the forehead.

"That's it," Trill continued. "Carry on, you lot. Bye then." And the fairy suddenly looked around, shocked, back to being himself again, and seeing, obviously, a lot of his fellow fairies all doing the same. "Oh," he said. "What did I miss?"

"Quite a lot," said Lizzie. She could see that Zoya, who'd found Jas, was looking bewildered. "I'll explain who that was in detail soon. If there is a soon." She looked back up to the sky, and saw that the angel, now fully formed, was heading down toward them again, to vast cheering from the gathered believers.

It was going to ask them. It was going to ask them the question and they were going to answer it, and it was going to somehow use that gathered belief and bring the world, the universe as they knew it, to a close.

"What can we do?" said Zoya. "I want to kick its arse. I think maybe I can now. But where do I even start?"

"Do magic, Mummy," said Jas.

"What Judith . . . what that old woman speaking through Trill said," Lizzie said. "Make it up. And—" She looked around, a sudden idea in her head, and saw that the fairies had now gathered with Trill, were looking both pleased to see him and furious at the same time. "Do any of you still have one of those arrows?" she said.

"Yes," said one of the fairies, "but they're full of our blood, we don't understand what—"

"Let me handle that bit." She pointed at the angel. "You've got a target." She had a terrible feeling she didn't have time. The crowd were already chanting "yes." It would only take a moment for the angel to ask its question.

But just as Lizzie was thinking that, she was startled to see arrows exactly like the ones that had been fired at her suddenly embedding themselves all over the descending angel.

The crowd bellowed in fury. Lizzie and everyone else turned together to see what had done this.

Into the market square, on steeds that looked like the dreams of horses, made of wind and fire, here came Finn, whole again, in gleaming armour, and with him were a horde of fairies, firing arrows and yelling so fiercely that Lizzie felt the anger of the crowd turn immediately into terror.

And there, right at the front of them, pale as death, hanging on like she was about to fall from the saddle, was Autumn Blunstone.

"I owe you too," the familiar voice with the Irish accent had said. "Damn it."

And Autumn had woken like she'd once woken from an anaesthetic, only then she hadn't felt so pleased with herself and fearful at the same time. She'd woken in the saddle of something terrifying, which was galloping straight toward . . . and then through . . . the wall around the town. She'd only just about had time to realise that there was an army with her, an army of guards that felt like they'd been literally assembled out of thin air, their emotions yelling between them that they were confused, having been suddenly drawn from many places and many dreams, but also determined, because they were doing the new and sudden will of the king.

Autumn saw Lizzie ahead, saw her out of all things in the instant they burst into the reality of the marketplace. She saw a moment later what was overhead, and she understood that here was their enemy. In the same moment, the fairies got that too. They heard a message from the king and began to fire at blurring speeds. It felt desperate. It felt like they only had seconds. But they were surely doing this because this was the only weapon that could reach that thing. Why would arrows hurt it?

And indeed, the angel was batting aside their shafts.

Except . . . now it was flailing, landing on the ground by the church, but stumbling, nearly swatting aside the people who were running to it in adulation. It clutched for just the one or two arrows in its chest, the one or two that had been fired not by her fairies but by those with Lizzie, the one or two that . . . were filled with fairy blood.

And then Autumn saw Lizzie step forward to say something to the angel.

———————

Lizzie had never been so scared. But also she had never

been so certain of her purpose. "You've got the fairy blood in you," she called up to the angel, over the angry shouts of the human beings all around. "So the control system has got to you, too, right? If it works on fairies and humans, it'll work on whatever you are. So now you believe completely in the aims of the project, don't you?"

That actually got a few cheers from the onlookers.

"Of course . . . I . . ." The warm voice had started to sound angry, flustered.

"You actually believe that the purpose of what you're doing is to bring eternal peace and justice. So. I have a question. Can you actually deliver that? Can you get it done? Or have you just been lying to everybody?"

The angel gave out an anguished howl.

"And if you've just been lying to everyone, now you believe in the project, don't you think you should tell us? Don't you think what you're really going to do is against the aims of the project? Don't you think you should stop? Or are you able to lie to yourself too?" Lizzie watched as the angel felt, as she did, the belief of the crowd falter with every grimace it made. It was fighting its own instantly grown conscience. It was at war with itself in exactly the way she now wasn't. She glanced over to Autumn and saw that her friend was looking at her with new appreciation.

Suddenly the angel stood straight once more. "No,"

said the voice of David Cummings. "Okay, so you've inconvenienced the boss, but I've taken direct control now, the plan is still on, enough of this lot still believe, so all I have to do is ask—"

But then Zoya yelled something Lizzie couldn't understand.

———

Zoya had suddenly understood that Lizzie had made her play, and Autumn was looking out of it, and that the fate of the universe was up to her. So she'd thought of her mum, thought of a few of the Ukrainian words for anything fairytale that she'd always used, and, shouting them, had grabbed hold of the land, from horizon to horizon.

She'd staggered for a moment, astounded that had worked. She looked down and saw Jas looking calmly back up at her, acknowledging with the barest of expressions the extremity of what her mum was doing. Zoya's mum hadn't lived long enough to meet Jas. Zoya knew she'd be proud to see her. She hoped she was, somehow, proud to see this.

Heaving like she was holding a weight in a cartoon, Zoya, aware that now everyone around her was watching, aware that if she dropped the world, well . . . that would be bad, wouldn't it?

"Now," said David Cummings, "let's carefully consider our options here."

And Zoya knew then that she had him by the balls. But how did she finish this? Oh. Right. What that old woman inside the fairy had said. Make it up. "Expellium fu . . . dgeoffium!" she bellowed, stumbling verbally and literally at the moment she realised Jas could hear her.

She pulled on the horizon as she shouted.

The angel went flying like he'd had a carpet dragged from under him. He spun for a second as a barrage of emotions including doubt and ridicule hit him. But it was the immense loss of control that Zoya could feel in that instant that did for him. It was what Cummings, in his last second bid to keep a lid on things, had been trying to avert.

The angel tried to right itself for a moment. It failed.

The angel exploded.

———————

Autumn staggered over to where Lizzie stood with Zoya, as what could only be described as pieces of angel fell all around them. She could feel that the wall around the town had vanished in the same instant the angel had lost control. "Hey," she said.

Lizzie embraced her. "You came back."

"It was . . . a journey," said Autumn. "I'll tell you about it later. With cocktails. Oh my God." She went over to where Luke was fallen to the ground, looking anguished. It was a look he shared with a lot of the people who were picking themselves up, surprised and startled to be helped to their feet by fairies.

"I believed it," he said to her. "All of it. I let you down."

"You never let her down," said Lizzie, helping him to stand. "You're only human and you did everything you could. And she loves you and you love her. Right?"

"Right," said Luke, laughing, like Autumn now found herself doing, at how direct Lizzie could be. When she wanted to be.

"Mistress," said a voice behind Autumn.

Autumn turned to see Zoya was on one knee, bowing to her, Jas laughing beside her. "Oh my God," said Autumn, "don't do that." She hauled her to her feet, Jas helping.

"Well, I gather I am meant to be your apprentice, yes?"

"That's fine, I saw what you did, I'm assuming I missed a lot, but no, I never called Judith anything and I don't want you calling me anything either."

"I don't know," said Luke. "Kind of horny."

"And that guilt and uncertainty lasted how long?"

Trill came over, a look of immense relief and pleasure

on his face. "I can feel, once again, the presence of the king. I am returned to my previous state. Do I take it that the war is over?"

"It's over all right," said Finn, marching up in his armour, flexing his fingers as if he was still trying this new body on for size. "And this lot won it. Oh, dispose of my other bits quickly," he said to Autumn. "You can't keep copies of me."

"I wouldn't want to," said Autumn, hugging Luke's arm.

"Sure you wouldn't," said Finn.

The red-faced man who'd been shouting a lot earlier strutted over, looked between them all, and adjusted his tie. "Mistakes were made," he said. "I believe we should all move on together. Welcome to Earth." And he extended his hand. To Trill.

Trill stepped forward and smiled at the hand.

Autumn led the others away, pleased to hear Finn, behind them, encouraging Trill to go ahead and be a diplomat, because after all there wasn't a prince anywhere nearby. "I think I made some suggestions to the king," she said, "about where we all go from here."

Epilogue

LIZZIE AND AUTUMN did indeed talk about everything over cocktails, and then at the Vicarage, with strong, sweet tea. Autumn, feeling that she had her best friend back, asked her what it was that had disturbed their friendship so much. Lizzie told her she didn't really remember.

Zoya, having negotiated quite a pay rise from what Judith had been getting, because, Autumn figured, she supposed she was hardly going to pick someone else, had come to work at Witches. She'd also proved herself to be an excellent apprentice. It'd be a long time before she could deliberately do anything as spectacular as what adrenaline and improvisation had allowed against the angel. But she was very interested and willing to learn. And, with a bunch of old books her mum had left her, she significantly increased Autumn's occult library.

The extra costs of having her around would, Autumn discovered, be more than met by the increased interest in all things magical the locals were expressing. What had previously been denial had now become acceptance. So there were at least a few customers around, actually buying things, most of the time. Carrie Anne Christopher, who'd led a small army of local nonbelievers back through the wall as soon as it had fallen, had also been in the lead of coordinating local response to the enormous media presence that had descended on the town. There was, after all, grieving to be done, whatever the supernatural background, the "impossible stuff," as everyone started to call it. The townsfolk of Lychford swiftly learned to simply agree with the pet theory of whoever was interviewing them. Autumn suspected that serious military people of some kind had been nosing around too. They probably weren't so easy to repel. And there were some, well, eccentric enthusiasts who'd just about moved in and were here for the long haul, helping the local economy and cluttering up her shop. Still, in the end, while the grief of families was taken on by Lizzie, the true story was whispered by the locals in the pubs and the parts of it that were impossible became a media sensation for a while, and then eventually ceased to be. Because they were impossible. The name of the town would be known forever now, but only in certain circles. As ever.

This acceptance of the supernatural among the locals, though, had, in a wonderful way, extended to an acceptance of Autumn herself. The first time she'd ventured

back into the Plough after "the incident," Rob the landlord had looked around his regulars, gone to the door
and locked it, then gruffly told her her money was no
good here, and that drinks would be free to her, always.
And she'd found, and this had made her start crying, that
everyone in the pub had started to applaud her.

Autumn supposed, in her more cynical moments, that
a lot of the town's inhabitants had opted to applaud
rather than apologise. But she'd take it.

———————

In the last minutes of Halloween, Zoya Boyko, having
been able, for the first time in her life, to pay for a babysitter, found herself standing by what the other two called
the well in the woods, surrounded by supernatural beings. She'd been introduced to the well a few days earlier,
when Autumn had decided that, whether or not Zoya
had been sort of naturally initiated when the power of the
land had sorted out its book-keeping error, they should
really go through with the ceremony.

Autumn had been busy with Finn arriving at all times
of day and night with many messages from his father. It
had all led to this. Standing around the well, listening for
the distant bells of Lizzie's church, stood Lizzie herself,
Autumn, Finn, representing his father, Cummings, back

in human form, representing his boss, and many other extraordinary figures, what she would have called demon and gnomes and sprites and pixies. Though she'd advised that not many of those names were accepted by the nations themselves. Autumn was holding a document, on parchment, and a quill pen. On the document was written the tortuous new agreement that would be all that would keep the supernatural nations at peace with each other.

"No more borders," Cummings sighed. "No wonder the boss has gone back to sleep. Even being an all-powerful angel bored him a bit. But this? What will we all do?"

"Bicker," said Finn. "Instead of frigging invading each other's collective consciousnesses."

"Prince," said Autumn, a warning note in her voice. "But Mr. Cummings is correct. Under the agreement there'll be regular meetings of leaders, committees and subcommittees. And a truth and reconciliation commission."

"Bureaucracy instead of mythology."

"Exactly," said Lizzie. "Have you read the small print?"

"Actually, no. The boss told me, before he turned in, to just come along and sign whatever it was. So there wasn't really any need for me to spend my valuable time doing that."

"Thought not," said Autumn.

They all reacted as the sound of the church bells chiming midnight sang across the clear night air. "All Saints' Day," said Lizzie.

"The end of Samhain," added or corrected Autumn.

"The day," said Lizzie, "when the powers of... other... go back to their places and we go back to ours. The day for new starts."

With a flourish, Autumn signed the document and handed it to Finn. He signed, too, and handed it to the gnome beside him. Finally, having passed around the circle, the signed document got to Cummings, who tiredly swiped his signature across it with a ballpoint and tossed it back to Autumn. "Well, then—" He was about to turn to go.

"Clause eighty-seven," said Finn, holding up the paper so he could squint at it.

"I can't see from there," said Cummings. With a roll of his eyes at being forced to do so, he stepped forward and bent to look at the level Finn was holding the paper.

Which was when Autumn produced from behind a tree an enormous broadsword and cut his head off with one swipe.

The head bounced off. Making all the supernatural beings who *had* read the small print nod approvingly.

"I think," said Autumn, putting the sword down again, "his boss felt that was an acceptable concession."

"He'll be back," said Finn. "Slightly inconvenienced. But oh, that was satisfying."

"For me too," said Autumn.

"I think," said Lizzie, "that Judith would approve."

Zoya decided, as the three of them walked home through the woods, that she was going to have to learn a lot more about this Judith.

———

The following June, in St. Martin's church, presided over by a delighted Lizzie, Autumn married Luke.

The happy couple had a full church. Which, to Lizzie's continuing joy, wasn't an odd occurrence these days. Autumn wore a green wedding dress, which had taken some finding. Lizzie's sermon was about how much she loved these two, how much they'd done for the town, and how she'd had to use marker pen on the bottom of Luke's shoes because his best man from the college had written some very rude things on them for when he kneeled down in front of the congregation.

They went off on honeymoon to Canada. Where, Lizzie was sure, they would find some sort of supernatural menace. And hopefully ignore it.

Lizzie watched them drive off in the white limo through the marketplace, both of them singing, actually singing, although it did seem to be different songs. Zoya, who looked as uncomfortable in pink bridesmaid frills as Jas looked delighted, was now trusted to run the shop while the owner was away. She and Lizzie had been spending a lot of time together lately. And she'd stopped calling her "reverend."

"So, Lizzie," she said now, "all back to yours after?"

Lizzie did bring a few back. And there were a few toasts for the happy couple, who'd texted from the airport to say Lizzie wouldn't believe what those with magical senses would encounter at Heathrow. Eventually, because Zoya was making the most of, and this was still rare for her, engaging a babysitter, all that remained were her and Lizzie, sitting up late with glasses of whiskey.

"So," said Zoya, looking at her over the rim of her glass with really quite a piercing gaze. "Are you ever going to come out to Autumn?"

Lizzie was proud of herself for not even disturbing the surface of her own drink. She'd kind of expected the question. She let her gaze meet Zoya's. And let it stay there. "Perhaps at my own wedding," said Lizzie Blackmore.

About the Author

Lou Abercrombie

PAUL CORNELL has written episodes of *Elementary, Doctor Who, Primeval, Robin Hood,* and many other TV series, including his own children's show, *Wavelength.* He's worked for every major comics company, including his creator-owned series *Saucer State* for IDW and *This Damned Band* for Dark Horse, and runs for Marvel and DC on *Batman and Robin, Wolverine,* and *Young Avengers.* He's the writer of the Lychford rural fantasy novellas from Tordotcom Publishing. He's won the BSFA Award for his short fiction, an Eagle Award for his comics, a Hugo Award for his podcast, and shares in a Writer's Guild Award for his *Doctor Who.* He's the cohost of *Hammer House of Podcast.*

TOR·COM

Science fiction. Fantasy. The universe.

And related subjects.

*

More than just a publisher's website, *Tor.com*
is a venue for **original fiction, comics,** and
discussion of the entire field of SF and fantasy,
in all media and from all sources. Visit our site
today—and join the conversation yourself.